**Don't miss Jenna Mindel's
delightful Regencies**

Miranda's Mistake

"Another fabulous story from Miss Mindel, the queen of romance. Her tale of love has a wonderful plot, desire, and a longing ache for true love to conquer." —Under the Covers

The Captain's Secret

"Secrets, traitors to the crown, action, and danger add up to one of the most delightful books I have enjoyed this year! Very, highly, and thoroughly recommended!" —Huntress Reviews

Labor of Love

"A delicious blend of gentle humor and poignant heartache." —*Romantic Times Book Club Magazine*

Blessing in Disguise

"A delightful romance . . . true reading pleasure." —Jo Beverley

"Warm, witty, and deliciously romantic—a splendid debut!" —Gail Eastwood

Kiss of the Highwayman

Jenna Mindel

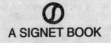

A SIGNET BOOK

SIGNET
Published by New American Library, a division of
Penguin Group (USA) Inc., 375 Hudson Street,
New York, New York 10014, U.S.A.
Penguin Books Ltd, 80 Strand,
London WC2R 0RL, England
Penguin Books Australia Ltd, 250 Camberwell Road,
Camberwell, Victoria 3124, Australia
Penguin Books Canada Ltd, 10 Alcorn Avenue,
Toronto, Ontario, Canada M4V 3B2
Penguin Books (N.Z.) Ltd, Cnr Rosedale and Airborne Roads,
Albany, Auckland 1310, New Zealand

Penguin Books Ltd, Registered Offices:
80 Strand, London WC2R 0RL, England

First published by Signet, an imprint of New American Library,
a division of Penguin Group (USA) Inc.

First Printing, March 2004
10 9 8 7 6 5 4 3 2 1

 REGISTERED TRADEMARK—MARCA REGISTRADA

Printed in the United States of America

PUBLISHER'S NOTE
This is a work of fiction. Names, characters, places, and incidents either are
the product of the author's imagination or are used fictitiously, and any
resemblance to actual persons, living or dead, business establishments,
events, or locales is entirely coincidental.

For Karen, Kathy, and Sarah—
Thank you for your encouragement and inspiration.

Prologue

December 1818
London

*B*rian Warren, now Lord Cherrington, Earl of Cherring, sat cooling his heels outside the office of the Home Secretary. After spending weeks in London paying his deceased brother's debts, before Christmas, Brian was no closer to knowing the identities of those responsible for Charles' death than when he had first come home from India. Brian hounded Bow Street day after day. He finally sought out a higher authority by obtaining an audience with Lord Sidmouth, to whom Bow Street ultimately reported. Brian was fairly burning with frustration.

A man with fine features and thinning gray hair stuck his head out of Sidmouth's office. "Lord Cherrington?" he asked.

Brian hesitated a moment then stood. He had not yet grown accustomed to being addressed as lord, his brother's title. It sounded odd. "Yes."

"I am Lord Sidmouth, do come in."

Brian bowed slightly before shaking the man's extended hand. Once inside the office, Lord Sidmouth gestured for him to sit down. Brian dropped into the chair, and his leg twitched. He was not accustomed to sitting patiently, and he had waited longer than he could bear. Lord Sidmouth sat down across from him with his folded hands atop his desk. Brian stared a moment at Sidmouth's long white fingers with nary a scratch or bit of dirt beneath the nails. It was obvious. Sidmouth was a man of paper instead of action. How bitter the thought.

"Now then, let us get straight to the heart of the matter," Lord Sidmouth said. His stare was direct, clear, and strong despite an outwardly weak appearance. "You have inquired repeatedly about the robbery which resulted in the loss of your brother's life."

"What is being done?" Brian asked.

"We have every available Runner in London working on catching the band of highwaymen."

"But you have not captured any of them?" Brian had received frequent updates from his daily visits.

"Regrettably, no. They are fast and clever. And by the way, have become romanticized by the female contingent of the *ton*. I do believe their antics will serve to draw many this Season."

Brian rose from his seat. "How can the murder of a peer be construed as romantic!"

Lord Sidmouth politely gestured for Brian to calm himself. "I truly believe your brother's death an accident. In fact his—rather, *your* servants explained it as such. For the most part there has been no physical harm done to either servants or nobility at these holdups. The common element between the victims is their wealth and high-social standing."

Brian shook his head, ready to argue. "Regardless of what my servants have said, these men caused my brother's death." He gritted his teeth. This was absurd! It made his blood boil to think the authorities did not appear overly worried about these cutthroats.

Brian suppressed his sarcastic urge to berate their efforts and took a deep breath. "How long has this been going on?"

Lord Sidmouth leaned back in his chair as if he had not a care in the world, his hands gently resting in his lap. "There have always been instances of crime in London, Lord Cherrington. Although you are new to the city, I must assure you that I am not a man to sit idly by."

Brian returned to his seat. The steel glint in Lord Sidmouth's eye revealed that perhaps he was not a man to be taken lightly. He was, in fact, deadly serious.

"This particular sort of robbery by this group started late in the year. The incidents were far and few between, so we did not realize at first that they were one and the same. The group's actions have increased on several roads leading into London. They disappear without a trace. Even though they brazenly commit their crimes in broad daylight. We cannot find anyone willing or able to turn one of the fellows in. These thieves dress in dark clothes covered with greatcoats that are neither shabby nor poorly made. Stealing jewels or anything of worth from their victims, they leave the ladies with nothing more than a token kiss of appreciation. These men may, in fact, be gentlemen."

"You are joking." Brian thought the idea preposterous that gentlemen would resort to such measures.

"Lord Cherrington, I am not in the least amused. Bow Street must keep quiet about it, for now. If this is a ruse perpetrated by a bunch of bored men of breeding, we must tread carefully. We must have absolute proof before pulling them in."

Brian chewed the end of his thumbnail. An idea took form and shape in his mind. "What if I were to help you obtain such proof?"

"How?"

"By becoming one of them."

Lord Sidmouth's eyes gleamed. "Then I shall put you in contact with John Stafford. He is the chief clerk of Bow Street and is quite used to undercover operations."

Chapter One

March 1819
North of London

Artemis Rothwell pulled the heavy wool blanket closer. She looked out of the carriage window with wary eyes. The large groom her father had sent as protection rode his horse next to them, keeping watch for footpads. He was powerfully built and wore a scowl that frightened many a man.

"Is he still there?" her stepmother, Lady Rothwell, asked without looking up from her needlework.

"Yes. Do you think we might see the highwaymen Miranda wrote to us about?" Artemis peeked out of the window once more.

"I certainly hope not. We are fortunate that your father did not cancel your come-out after hearing of such tales."

Artemis was relieved that after much pleading and stamping of feet, her father had finally given over, allowing them to make the journey to London. It had taken quite a week or more to win her stubborn father's approval.

In addition to the formidable groom acting as sentinel, a lady's maid, a coachman along with another groomsman, and a tiger traveled with them. They were hardly alone and vulnerable, but they were a bit late.

Artemis had her measurements sent directly to her stepmother's dearest friend, Miranda, now Lady Ashbourne. Miranda's mantua maker would no doubt make up for the lost time. Never caring much about what she wore, Artemis knew her gown choices had been placed in capable hands, but she had to own that she looked forward to trying on the new dresses for final fittings once she arrived.

She sighed.

Fittings and new dresses brought back clear memories of the hunting party her parents held at Rothwell Park this past autumn in time for the Quorn hunt. Miranda had arrived early in order to give Artemis much needed polish and instruction on how to go on among members of the *ton*. Artemis actually cringed when she thought of how poorly she had acted.

Lord Ashbourne had been one of several single gentlemen invited by her parents with hopes of making a match. Artemis had never held interest in marriage, but once she realized that Ashbourne was considered a veritable prize by every dainty young miss present, Artemis encouraged his openly pronounced suit and hoped to come out the victor. She had desperately wanted to beat the high and mighty beauties at their own game.

Artemis leaned against the leather squabs of the carriage and closed her eyes. She should have known better than to accept Ashbourne's offer when she knew there was an attraction between him and Miranda. But of course, being headstrong and insecure, she ignored all warning signs. She had allowed her father to make the announcement of her engagement. It was mere days later that she jilted Ashbourne because she knew he loved Miranda.

But that was after Miranda was nearly killed in an attempt to catch Artemis and keep her stunt of riding in the Quorn hunt dressed as a man from being discovered. Artemis had come close to ruining her family's good name!

If only she could turn back the clock and relive those brief weeks. She would have behaved differently, and then perhaps the thought of facing the *ton* would not be so daunting. Ashbourne and Miranda had put all of it behind them, but Artemis anxiously wondered what response she would receive when she met those same guests from the hunting party in Town?

She leaned forward to let down the window just a slight crack. The air was cool, but the sun shone brightly and the carriage wheels droned on as they moved swiftly along the North Road toward London.

Her father had cleverly planned to come later on horseback with the jewels and other valuables needed for a Season. Lord Ashbourne arranged to accompany him, and the two would no doubt make it through without rousing the highwaymen's notice.

Miranda had written to them about the latest rage to hit London. Being kissed and robbed by a mysterious band of highwaymen had become a girlish fantasy come true. So far, no one had come to any physical harm. This made the prospect of being held up all the more appealing to many young ladies. Miranda had further described in her letters how she had heard tales of young misses staging carriage breakdowns in hopes of receiving a visit from the masked men. Artemis could not help but find the possibility of meeting these infamous highwaymen intriguing, even though she thought such antics foolish in the extreme.

Miranda was sponsoring her introduction to the *ton*. Despite the worries that plagued Artemis when surrounded by other young ladies, she had to own an almost equal measure of excitement. Any reluctance to have a Season fell by the wayside once the trip was underway. A Rothwell did not cower in the country!

Even so, Artemis looked forward to seeing the sights. She refused to think about comparing herself to the other ladies making their bows. There was simply no reason to fret about anything that might weaken her resolve to make her parents proud by making her curtsy to society. The nearer they drew to the city, the more agitated she became with a rush of conflicting emotions. Whatever this spring held for her, she hoped she was ready for it.

Nearly a quarter hour had passed when Artemis jerked forward as the carriage came to an abrupt halt. Fear mixed with anticipation trickled down her spine, making her shiver. She looked at her stepmother, who had paled considerably.

"Stand and deliver," a shout rang out.

Her heart beat faster as she peered out the window. Their groom was nowhere to be seen. Four men dressed in black greatcoats and masks, brandishing pistols, surrounded their coach.

"Be still and listen. We do not wish anyone ill will," one of them yelled up to the coachman.

Marna, her maid, slumped to the floor in a dead faint.

"Mama, what will we do?" Artemis hissed.

"Whatever they ask of us."

They heard telltale scratches upon the roof and some thumping along with the coachman's expletives. Then there was silence.

Artemis reached to grab hold of her stepmother's hand, but she was trying to rouse Marna. And then the door opened.

"Ladies." A tall masked man bowed before them as if he were requesting their favor for a dance. "If you please, step out of the carriage."

"Our maid is not well, as you can see. Perhaps we should remain inside." Her stepmother's fear was only evident in that she had spoken much too loud for the close surroundings.

Artemis watched her beloved stepmother and the Highwayman to see who would give over first. The slight thinning of her stepmother's lips was the only clue that she was furious, but the Highwayman did not falter. He merely extended his gloved hand to her. Her stepmother finally took it and stepped out of the carriage.

Then he reached in for Artemis. "Your turn, my dove," he teased.

She refused his hand and stepped out on her own.

"A feisty minx," he said with a chuckle. Then he stooped low to enter the carriage.

Artemis stood close to her stepmother. They clung to each other and waited for what might happen next.

After searching the insides, the tall man jumped out. "It's completely clean. There is nothing of value in there."

A man, who could only be the leader of the bandits, walked with an exaggerated swagger until he stood directly in front of them. "Well, well, well," he said. "You have outsmarted us by traveling empty-handed."

Artemis shuddered at the hint of menace beneath the cultured soft voice.

He leaned closer to her stepmother, whose chin lifted high with disdain. "I must claim something to make this fuss worthwhile." He gestured flamboyantly toward the scene around them. "Now, then, my lady, perhaps a kiss to reward my efforts."

"Do not dare," her stepmother said with such haughty contempt that Artemis thought the man might actually back away.

But he did not. He pulled her stepmother's face in both hands and kissed her soundly upon the lips. She immediately jerked back and raised her arm in order to slap him, but the bandit was quicker.

He grabbed hold of her wrist. "Tsk, tsk, tsk. That is not at all polite." He proceeded to gently pull the leather glove from her stepmother's hand. "For shame, it appears that you were remiss in hiding your ring." He pulled the wedding ring from her slender finger.

"Please, do not. That ring has never left my finger since my husband gave it to me in marriage."

Artemis nearly groaned aloud. *How could she have forgotten to take off the Rothwell ring?* It was her mother's and her grandmother's and even her great-grandmother's before her. It was worth a small fortune!

Artemis felt fury burn through her veins as she watched her stepmother struggle with her composure. Artemis knew that when her father found out about this, he was going to be cross as crabs. It shredded her heart to see her stepmother bravely hold back the tears that threatened to fall.

She had to do something.

Seconds ticked by, but they felt like hours. Artemis spied the Leader's pistol strapped to his hip. It would be relatively easy to take it. Quickly, she snatched the weapon and pointed it straight at the man still holding her stepmother's wrist.

"Give it back," Artemis growled. She stepped away from the two of them, in order to get out of the Leader's reach. She backed against the carriage to give her strength and remain standing. Her legs shook, but her arm raised with the pistol remained steady.

"Artemis, no!" her stepmother looked even more frightened.

Artemis had miscalculated her chance for success when the Leader twisted her stepmother around into his embrace in order to shield himself.

"Let her go!" Artemis cocked the pistol. She had only one shot.

"Listen to your mother, my giantess," the Leader said calmly. "Drop the pistol. You cannot wish to hit her by mistake."

Artemis hesitated, but she would not back down. Not yet. "You wish to try my aim, sir?" She stared into the man's eyes that had now grown cold with anger and something close to disgust.

"It is quite unnatural for a woman to have a true aim," he sneered. "And so I ask you, are you more woman or man? From your gigantic appearance, I cannot tell."

His words, meant to cut her, had the desired effect. Her confidence faltered then completely died when she heard two of his cohorts sniggering with suppressed laughter. She dropped her arm, still holding the pistol.

The tall man inched his way toward her. He wrapped his arms around her, gently grabbing the loaded pistol to keep her from raising the weapon again.

He was tall indeed. She had to look up. His eyes were so blue that she was momentarily blinded by their intensity. He cradled her in an intimate embrace as he pulled the gun out of her hand. The warmth of his body seeped into her fear-chilled being, and she swore, against her will, that she melted. She knew that he had noticed her reaction because a smile tugged at his shapely lips.

He pulled her closer.

Dear Heaven, he was going to kiss her!

By all that was Holy, she welcomed it. Her eyelids grew heavy when his lips touched hers for the briefest of sweet kisses. She groaned with disappointment when he ended it.

"I will return the ring to you," the tall man whispered into her ear.

The Leader, who still held her stepmother, suddenly spun her about and let her go. "Come, Romeo, we tarry too long," he said with barely concealed contempt.

In moments they were gone into the woods as quietly as they had come out from them. Artemis' weakened knees gave out, and she dropped to the ground.

Her stepmother rushed to her side and wrapped her arms about her. "Artemis you could have been hurt. Whatever possessed you to do such a thing?" She helped her to stand.

Artemis could not speak. Her lips blazed with heat left by the tall dark highwayman that had promised to right the wrong done to them. But she could not trust the word of an outlaw!

Suddenly, she felt like a complete fool.

"Come, we must untie the others and find our groom." Her stepmother pulled at her hand. "Are you all right, dear? You have had quite a scare."

"We must get back that ring," she murmured, but her stepmother was already climbing up the coach to attend to the servants.

Artemis ran her fingertips over her lips. She feared she would never be quite all right until the Rothwell ring was returned.

Brian scurried through the trees, alone. It had been his third holdup after infiltrating the band of gentlemen playing at criminals. Each and every one of them was a gentleman. It had taken him weeks of hanging about disreputable establishments and various haunts to finally find out how to join them. Sheer luck had brought him upon a fallen note in a gaming hell that had a time and a place marked upon it.

Not willing to overlook anything out of the ordinary, Brian went to the designated place and skulked about in the shadows. When he saw three men with their faces covered enter an abandoned barn on Tothill Fields, he knew he had discovered them.

Fortunately, Brian had carried a mask of his own that he put on when he entered. He disguised his voice by making it deeper and rougher. He had showed the Leader the note he had found, and he expressed his desperate need for ready funds. He said that he had followed their history of holdups with the desire to join them.

Unbelievably, he was accepted. He had quietly given the Leader a false name, but one Brian knew well. When his brother, Charles, had wanted to escape their father's knowing searches, Charles used an identity he had made up. Upon reviewing Charles' finances with the Cherrington solicitors, they had stumbled upon this made-up rogue.

John Fellows was a fictitious character with a bank account and even a London address. After embarking on his plan to infiltrate the highwaymen, Brian kept up the pretense. He even paid a month's rent at the Cheapside flat this John Fellows was supposed to have inhabited.

Brian had been put through his paces to prove his loyalty. His name and address had been checked thoroughly by the Leader. The other two men knew nothing about him. Nor did he know them.

The Leader had sent him on small errands, and had him commit thefts and even forced him to hold his hand over a flame until his flesh burned. There was a delicate trust within the group even though no one knew the identity of the other. Only the Leader, an engaging chap despite the iron reign he held on his temper, knew his followers.

Brian had to own it was an ingenious way to organize. With such knowledge came complete control, and the leader exercised a good measure over them all, especially when they split the booty after their robberies. The Leader always took a larger portion.

None of the men complained. In fact, Brian thought the men were too cheery about it. Lord Sidmouth's warning about men of breeding bored with life rang very close to home. These men enjoyed their charade like a bunch of youngsters at Eton. After several meetings, Brian knew they were in it merely for amusement. The fact that his brother had paid a dear price for their *sport* deepened his resolve. He would uncover them and hand them over to Lord Sidmouth before the Season was over.

He reached his horse that was tied to an ancient oak near a stream. His mount, rented for this afternoon's escapade, whickered a soft greeting.

Brian rubbed the gelding's nose. "Another interesting day with little information." He sighed. He had learned nothing more of these men than when he had first joined them. Small talk was prohibited, else the Leader threatened to reveal their identity. Not a word had been uttered about the only injury to one of their victims, the only death—Charles.

He quickly took off his greatcoat and mask and stuffed them into a pouch behind his saddle. This had been their first holdup with no bounty. Although the Leader still had that woman's ring. The ring he promised he would return.

Her name was Artemis. He could think of none better for the tall Amazon who had bravely defied them. She had been magnificent in her calm fury. Once he had her in his arms, he knew better. She quaked and trembled with fear. It had been all he could do not to soothe her. Instead, he had kissed her, in keeping with the band's trademark. And he rather enjoyed it. Had it been another place under different circumstances, he would have taken time enough to ensure that his kiss had been returned.

He mounted his gelding and made his way back to Town. Soon the Season would commence. He needed to work on these gentlemen thieves from within the world of society. He had tried to listen carefully to voices, but it had proved difficult. They hardly spoke. Only the Leader was vocal, and yet he'd bet the voice was disguised somehow. The Leader must be his focus. Brian felt it deep in his gut that it was the Leader who had killed Charles. The others did not have the stomachs for it.

Artemis and her stepmother walked up the steps as the door opened.

"Finally, you have come." Miranda welcomed them into her townhouse with warm embraces. "I was beginning to worry."

"Oh, Miranda, what we have been through," her stepmother said warily.

"Bea, do not say that the highwaymen stopped you." The look of horror on Miranda's face was undeniable.

"They took Mama's ring," Artemis said. "We have to get it back."

Miranda looked down at her friend's hand. "Oh no, Bea. Your wedding ring? The Rothwell ring?"

"Papa's going to be furious," Artemis added.

"Your father is not going to know," her stepmother said. "Not now at least. He will never let you stay if he thinks we were robbed. He will call off your Season and go looking for the scoundrels which would no doubt get him killed."

Miranda looked concerned. "Bea, are you quite certain?"

"Yes. How about some tea? We could both use it."

Miranda's cheeks reddened with shame. "My goodness. Come, sit in front of the fire, and I will have tea brought at once. You must tell me everything."

Artemis nearly laughed. Her stepmother had at one time been Miranda's governess, and it was obvious that Miranda still took her counsel. Even though her stepmother was rattled, she still handed out instruction. It was as it had always been with the three of them, and Artemis relaxed, realizing there was never going to be awkwardness between her and Miranda.

Artemis wondered if Miranda would be comfortable keeping this bit of news quiet, especially from her husband, Lord Ashbourne. But her stepmother knew what she was doing. She had been managing her father successfully for the past ten years. The story would no doubt be told, once the two of them were safely back at Rothwell Park. If they managed to retrieve the ring before her father knew it was missing, then all would be saved.

Artemis sat down in a comfortable chair by the hearth and leaned her head back. She felt like she had been swimming in a river against a fast current. She was exhausted.

"Artemis, are you sure you are well?" Her stepmother's voice intruded upon her thoughts. "Perhaps you should lie down."

"I am fine."

"But you must be tired. You stood up to those cads! And you seemed quite affected by that highwayman's kiss." Her stepmother had kept her humor, and she proved it with a saucy wink.

"You were kissed?" Miranda asked eagerly.

"So was Mama," Artemis said to keep the attention away from her. She was in no mood to discuss the tall Highwayman.

"A fresh-fresh faced young puppy that man was," her stepmother nearly spat. She turned to Miranda. "It was a different rascal who kissed me."

"Did you see his face?" Miranda asked. "How many were there?"

"No," her stepmother said. "There were four of them all told. They wore dark masks covering their faces. But something in the Leader's manner was very young and untried. It would not surprise me if these ruffians were nothing more than lads."

The tea cart arrived and Miranda poured. Once the cups were handed out, Miranda sat back down, ready to continue their coze. "I have heard rumors," she whispered, "that these men are in fact gentlemen."

Artemis and her stepmother gasped in shock.

Was the man who had kissed her a gentleman?

Artemis wondered. His voice sounded refined. But why would a gentleman turn to a life of crime? And how long would they be left uncaught to terrorize the countryside?

"I say, Artemis, what was the man like who kissed you?"

Artemis glanced quickly at her stepmother, who sipped her tea. "I do not recall," she fibbed. "It happened so fast."

"He was very tall, and I think he quite took her breath away," her stepmother teased. "I will lay odds that she did the same to him. Miranda, my daughter pulled a pistol upon them! But alas, her weapon was taken by the very man who left her with a kiss."

"Mama, please!"

Miranda gave her an encouraging smile. "I am sure you are not the only female whose head has been turned by a dashing highwayman."

"He was not dashing," Artemis protested. "And my head was not turned. But it is pounding, so if you will excuse me, I think I shall take up your offer to retire to my room before dinner."

Her stepmother's brow creased in concern. "I beg your forgiveness, dear, it has been a harrowing day for me as well. I do not mean to make light of it. I will check on you shortly."

Artemis bent down to kiss her stepmother's forehead. "I understand." She turned to their hostess. "No fuss is needed, Miranda. I know the way."

"Rest well, dear." Miranda settled back down into her chair, her feet pulled up underneath her.

*　　*　　*

Brian surveyed his newly purchased clothes with complete distaste. They were truly awful, but they would definitely disguise him.

"Are you sure about this?" Clancy, his assistant acting as valet, asked.

"Yes," Brian answered. It had been almost a week since the holdup, and in that time Brian had polished a plan of action to infiltrate society until it shone.

"Do you think any one of those blokes will let you get close to them?"

"That is not what I need. I need to appear ridiculous and remain invisible in my search of who these men are. I cannot appear anything like my real self. My identity as a highwayman cannot be discovered, not until I have proof for Lord Sidmouth's man, John Stafford."

"You're dicked in the nob, I say." Clancy hung up a lawn shirt in the adjoining dressing room. "The whole thing is a ramshackle."

Brian tried on one of the flamboyant waistcoats he had purchased. The violet silk with scarlet stripes did indeed look ridiculous. But it would all be worth it in the end. It had to be.

He washed his hands and stood back to examine himself in the cheval mirror. His hair had been trimmed this morning into a short cap with points of hair along his forehead called the Brutus. But his skin looked dark even after months in England. He dare not appear like a man who worked out of doors.

Brian rifled through the creams and perfumes he purchased until he found the small container of rice powder. Ladies used it to diminish freckles, and some men did too. He applied a generous amount and achieved his desire. His skin looked pale.

He had always thought of himself as too skinny. His slight build only helped him play the part of a fribble. With his ridiculously high shirt points and polished boots with tassels, he looked every inch a dandy. He practiced twirling his quizzing glass as he minced his way around the room. His ankle twisted, and he nearly fell to his knees. He recovered quickly if awkwardly. Sauntering was definitely a challenge.

Clancy laughed aloud at him. "Good God!"

Brian ignored Clancy's jabs. He turned on his heel and cocked his elbow in a feminine manner. He raised his voice and asked, "Come now, Clancy, don't you think I might snag myself a well-rounded bride while I'm here?"

More laughter. "Are you looking for funds or curves?"

"Why, both of course!"

Clancy sat upon a chair wiping the tears from his eyes. "I pity the lady who must cautiously dress so as not to clash with you."

" 'Tis a good thing, then, that white is still the color of choice among young ladies making their come-out."

"Those winkers will poke your eyes out if you do not use care when turning your head," Clancy advised.

Brian placed his new quizzing glass up to his eye. "I thought the higher the shirt collar, the better dressed the man."

Clancy suddenly turned serious. "Do be careful, my lord."

Brian was caught off guard. Addressed as lord solemnly by Clancy sobered him. They had been through many adventures in India and beyond, but never had Brian done anything like this. "I have the title to protect now, Clancy. I will do nothing to endanger or embarrass that, much good it will do after what Charles has done. Now, help me into my coat. I'm off to Boodle's."

With a pat on the back from Clancy, Brian left the Cherrington townhouse in Mayfair, cane in hand. He walked the few blocks to his brother's club. He was the recipient of several raised eyebrows as he passed, but all in all, Brian felt like he fit into the evening crowd.

He hesitated before entering the club. This was more difficult than he had imagined. He was nervous but determined to ferret out the gentlemen who posed as highwaymen. He owed it to his mother, who was grief-stricken from the loss of her eldest son. But even more so, he owed it to the memory of his father.

Perhaps he might finally make his father proud by finding the men responsible for Charles' death. With a deep breath, Brian pushed open the door and walked in.

Chapter Two

*H*e sat alone in his club, twirling the ring he took from the Rothwell woman between his fingers. The emerald was large and square cut, with rubies and sapphires surrounding it. It was an ancient piece, and one he'd wager was rare. It was not something he could unload quickly. He shoved it back in his pocket and waved for the waiter to bring him another bottle.

He was quickly tiring of this farce with the fools he'd taken in as highwaymen. And he did not trust the newcomer named John Fellows. But it did not matter, really. It was nearly time to bring his charade to a close before he got caught. His debts had long since been paid, but his thirst for revenge had not yet been quenched. It could not be until each of the gentlemen he had lured into this scheme had been socially ruined. He did not mind that he stole from many of the upper ten thousand—the very group he so longed to impress.

Brian entered Boodle's with a wary eye. He did his best to saunter toward the man in charge of the establishment. He gave his name and verified that his membership had been reinstated with the full payment of past dues. With all things in place, he raised his quizzing glass and ordered a light supper.

He quickly chose a table near a window. The place was not nearly as crowded as he had expected, but even so, several men took notice of him.

"I say," a man carrying a bottle of brandy along with two glasses approached him. "I could not help but overhear." The man cocked his head. "Lord Cherrington, might I join you?"

Brian cleared his throat before affecting a higher voice as he said. "Of course." He gestured toward the man to take a seat.

"George Clasby," the man said. "I knew a Lord Cherrington of Somerset. Are you perhaps his heir?" He extended his hand.

Brian remembered to shake limply. "I am Lord Cherrington, Earl of Cherring, and Charles' brother and heir."

Clasby looked shocked. "I beg your pardon for staring, but you are nothing like your brother in resemblance. He was an entertaining fellow, and I knew him well. My condolences."

Brian chuckled before answering truthfully, "You are indeed correct. I am nothing like Charles." Maintaining the high voice took effort.

"He mentioned he had a younger brother who was out of the country." Clasby paused, as if trying to remember.

"I have indeed been traveling on the Continent for some time," Brian supplied quickly. He wondered why this man had approached him. Was he simply curious about his brother's replacement? He was the same in stature as the Leader of the highwaymen he sought, but the voice wasn't right. But then again, the Leader disguised his somehow. Brian tried to relax.

"How long has it been since you were last in London?"

Brian's eyes narrowed instinctively. "Why do you ask?"

Clasby looked sheepish, as if he had offended. "No reason. You appeared a bit lost when you came in, and so I figured that I'd introduce myself, once I heard who you were. Besides, I was growing bored with the small group of men wagering on which ladies would repeat their Season this year from last. If you prefer that I take my leave."

"Pon rep, no." Brian held out his hand. He knew so little about the haute monde these days. He knew the basics. He knew the names of the best families. It had been two years since he had last been in England, and even longer for London. He could not afford to rule anyone out from being the villain he sought. "I did not intend to be rude. I have ordered a plate. Would you care to join me in a slab of roast?"

"I have yet to have my supper. Indeed, I will."

"Good," Brian said. "If I might be so bold, I would greatly appreciate any news you could share to bring me up to snuff with the *ton*."

Clasby laughed aloud. "Of course. In fact, tomorrow night I dine at the house of one of London's most respected matrons. A friend of mine recently

married her. Lady Ashbourne is the one to know if
you wish to move in the upper circle. You must come
with me."

Brian considered this. He needed to build connections, find out who was who. "Yes, I shall definitely
go with you."

"Mr. Clasby has sent a note that he is bringing a
gentleman to dine with us," Miranda announced to
her husband. "Since Rothwell has only just arrived
with you early this afternoon, do you think he will
mind?"

Artemis looked up from her book. "Papa will not
mind. He's given to the philosophy that the more is
always the merrier."

Ashbourne asked, "Did Clasby mention the
man's name?"

"Lord Cherrington. The new one."

"I don't know him." Ashbourne frowned.

"Neither do I," Miranda explained. "I met his
brother at a ball some years back. He rarely attended
society functions. I understand he was somewhat of
a rakehell."

Ashbourne's scowl only deepened.

"Do not look so grim, Evan," Miranda teased. "His
heir might very well be different."

Artemis did not miss the meaningful look Miranda
gave her husband. Lord Cherrington would be inspected as a possible suitor.

His brow cleared. "Well then, let us meet the new
Lord Cherrington."

"Artemis, you have not yet made your curtsy at

court, and already a gentleman caller is coming to dinner." Miranda, enormously happy with her marriage to Ashbourne, lived in a state of constant cheerfulness. She was convinced that Artemis need only find the right man and the same wedded bliss could be hers.

It was not a view shared by Artemis, although she was not truly opposed to the idea of marriage. She simply could not conceive of finding the depth of love that Miranda and Ashbourne shared. Artemis believed she would be quite content with strong affection and respect. Considering her great height, she would be fortunate to find a potential mate with whom she might cry friends and common interests. She had no illusions of fairy-tale love.

The idea of searching for one's true love during the Season was daunting. How could she possibly go about trying to find such a man? It was bad enough, knowing she stood over a head taller than the other young ladies making their bows this Season. To compete with them for the same gentlemen would only cause her undue stress.

"We shall see about this gentleman," Ashbourne said with an encouraging smile. He understood her shortcomings and tried his best to keep Miranda balanced about matchmaking.

"Even so, we shall have to pick out a suitable gown." Miranda grinned. "Come, Artemis, your mama is already above stairs changing for dinner. Let us get her opinion."

Artemis followed Miranda to the feminine bedchamber decorated in shades of pink that had been assigned to her. The large connecting dressing room was equally frivolous with small pink velvet chairs and a marble vanity.

"Hmmmm," Miranda purred. She browsed the various dresses. "What shall you wear?"

"What about the blue?" Artemis asked.

"Too formal for an informal dinner with friends." Miranda proceeded to flick aside each gown until she stopped with an approving nod. "This will be perfect."

Artemis agreed. The gown was made of dull gold silk with a wide sash and flounces of ivory. It would wear well for many occasions. "I rather like this one."

"Shall I have my maid do your hair?"

"Marna can fix my hair; she is used to it." Artemis sat down to look through her box of jewels.

"Very well," Miranda kissed the top of her forehead. "I will change and meet you in your mama's room. She will want to see you too."

Artemis went to work on her appearance with the help of her maid, Marna. Although she feigned indifference to the news of a gentleman coming to dinner, she had to own she felt a certain measure of excitement. Perhaps meeting a man in the safe and comfortable surroundings of Miranda's home with family present would make it easier to be herself. Tonight there would be no dainty young ladies to make her feel like a giant.

After Marna had finished the upswept style of her heavy hair, Artemis smoothed the folds of her dress. She was ready for her stepmother's inspection. She made her way to her parents' rooms and knocked softly.

"Come in," her father called out.

Artemis entered and twirled when her stepmother's eyes lit up with pride.

"Oh, Artemis, you look beautiful, does she not, Rothwell?"

Her father gave her a critical look, then his face split into a broad smile. "You do, my girl. Something has changed in you over these last few months. I cannot say exactly what it is, but only that I like the looks of it on you."

Artemis curtsied as Miranda had taught her. It was slightly less formal than what she would use at court, but even so, she had practiced it to perfection.

She felt as if she had indeed changed. She liked to think that she had grown up since riding in the Quorn to impress Lord Ashbourne last November.

When Miranda had almost been killed by a fall from her horse in an attempt to rescue Artemis from her own foolishness, Artemis knew she had to come to terms with who she was once and for all. No matter how much she balked, she was a lady, and it was high time she started acting as one. This Season marked a new beginning for her. Artemis Rothwell was determined to be comfortable in her own skin.

Since arriving in London over a week ago, she had been a pattern card of good behavior. She did not object to the gowns Miranda chose. She did not go into a huff over the dancing instructor that had been brought in to smooth her dance steps. She even tried her best to pour tea steadily, keep her napkin firmly on her lap, and dress her hair in a style befitting the daughter of a peer, instead of letting it fall loose about her shoulders like the hoyden she had been.

And, she had finally dropped the subject of the stolen ring. After searching several pawnshops and coming away with no sign of the ring, Artemis promised her stepmother to remain quiet. She did not breathe a word of it to her father. Miranda had miraculously refrained from telling her husband. Her stepmother reasoned that no doubt the criminals would hold onto it for a while. It was far too unique to trade it in so quickly after it had been taken.

Artemis had reluctantly agreed, but her mind continued to work furiously on ways she might get it back. She could not alert Bow Street until her parents left town, in order to keep her father ignorant of the theft. The Runners would no doubt question him, if a report was filed.

Her father, anxious to return to his land and new foals, agreed to attend only a few sessions of Parliament. Politics lacked the allure to keep him in London for more than a couple of weeks. But her parents promised to return at the end of the Season.

She would be on her own for the first time in her nineteen years of life. And by the end of the Season, she would have that ring!

Brian stepped out of Clasby's carriage. He minced up the steps to the main door of the townhouse in the middle of Mayfair that was less than a block from his own. In fact, he believed their back courtyards abutted one another.

He took a deep breath to steady his nerves. He was not completely adept at acting the dandy, but he knew there must be no question of who he might be. Clasby knocked on the door, and it was opened not by a butler or footman, but apparently by the lord himself.

"Ashbourne." Clasby gave him a wicked grin. "You look well cared for."

"And you are the wretch who spent Christmastide in Town."

"Didn't want to intrude upon the newlywed lovebirds."

Brian watched the good-hearted exchange between the men, who were obviously close friends.

"This is Lord Cherrington," Clasby finally said. "Lord Ashbourne."

"Pleased to make your acquaintance, Lord Ashbourne." Brian did not miss the raised brow or the quickly concealed look of incredulity on Asbourne's face.

"Lord Cherrington, welcome to my, er, well, my wife's home, actually."

"Married just four months ago," Clasby whispered loud enough for Ashbourne to hear.

"Congratulations are in order, then," Brian said with a wink.

"Indeed they are. And what are your feelings toward the hallowed state of matrimony?" Lord Ashbourne took Brian's gold-handled cane and leaned it against a wall in the large entryway.

Clasby tried to suppress a guffaw, but was unsuccessful.

Brian nearly choked on a bark of laughter rising in his throat. Ashbourne thought him a dashed backgammon player! He chose his words with care. "Considering that I am now the earl, I have given serious thought to creating heirs." It was the perfect reason for being in London. He must appear to be on the Marriage Mart. "My hope is to find a willing bride this Season," he managed with a serious expression even though his lips twitched at the corners.

Lord Ashbourne cast a quick glance at Clasby, who insolently smiled as if he had succeeded in bringing the perfect entertainment for the evening. "Ah, then I wish you well in your search."

"Thank you, Lord Ashbourne."

They entered the drawing room, where three ladies and another gentleman stood waiting. Their expressions immediately went blank when they saw him.

Brian raised his quizzing glass to his eye. The tall young lady dressed in gold was none other than the Amazon who had pulled a pistol on the Leader a week ago. He let his gaze feast upon her near perfect form. She was rounded where a woman should be. Her arms and neck were slender, and he imagined lithe long legs under the ivory flounces of her cone shaped skirt.

He smiled too broadly at his thoughts and turned his attention to Lord Ashbourne, who proceeded with the introductions. He made his bows to Lord Rothwell, the Amazon's father. He looked like he had taken a bite of a sour pickle, but managed a friendly welcome.

To Rothwell's brave wife, who had kept her dignity during the humiliating kiss she was forced to endure from the Leader, Brian deposited a generous kiss upon her hand. He repeated the gesture to Lady Ashbourne, under the watchful eye of her husband.

"Lord Cherrington, this is Miss Artemis Rothwell,

who enjoys her first Season this year," Lord Ashbourne said with a barely concealed tone of warning.

"Enchanted," he whispered with amazingly real
reverence. He made a leg then took her hand to his
lips for the briefest of kisses, since she pulled her
hand immediately away.

She looked amused by him and also a bit annoyed,
but there was no recognition. Good, he thought. She
had no idea who he was.

Lady Ashbourne intervened to keep the silence
that descended upon them from becoming awkward.
"Shall we make our way to the dining room?"

"Indeed," Lady Rothwell agreed.

Brian was impressed when dinner progressed into
a warm family-styled meal. Clasby caught them up
on society gossip as the Rothwells were newly arrived to Town and Lord Ashbourne, Brian found out,
had not been to London in nearly seven years.

"Do you reside in Town year-round, Lord Cherrington?" Lady Ashbourne asked.

He delicately ladled plum sauce over his duck.
"No. I have only just arrived after spending several
years abroad."

"I see," Lady Ashbourne said with a knowing nod.
The others looked relieved, as if his foreign travels
explained his outlandish appearance.

"I have moved into the Cherrington townhouse for
the Season, but my country estate is in Somerset. I
shall reside there mostly." And that was the complete
truth. Brian knew he was needed to oversee the sadly
unsupervised tenants. Charles' bailiff, who had also
served their father, had become lazy. The man had

made no improvements for far too long. There had been no crop rotation, no practice of leaving fields fallow, and several outbuildings had leaky roofs. The thought of how Cherring House and its dependents had been neglected made Brian seethe with irritation. His irresponsible brother had not done his duty.

He glanced at Artemis, who watched him. He had momentarily let his voice deepen. "Pon rep, if I do not return to London for the Season. It is the highlight of every year, *non*?" That earned him a sorry look from the Amazon.

"Will you attend Parliament?" Artemis asked quietly.

Brian felt like her question was a test, and he wanted to pass it. "Of course," he answered with a wink. " 'Tis my duty."

"My father's always thought it a waste of time," Artemis said with pride.

Brian had not answered correctly yet again. He obviously did not meet the standard of what Miss Rothwell thought a man should be. That she admired her father was quite clear.

Lord Rothwell blustered slightly, and an uncomfortable silence settled over the table. Such an admission should never be aired in front of a stranger who could spread the damaging statement.

Lord Ashbourne immediately came to the rescue. "This is my first session of Parliament. Rothwell, although he bristles at times, has promised to show me the ropes. Perhaps you might join us?"

"Yes, indeed," Rothwell added quickly. "My daughter tends to repeat some of my ranting." He patted his daughter's hand to assure her that no harm had been done.

"I would be honored." Brian appreciated the offer. Lord Ashbourne's wife smiled approvingly at her husband with an expression of pure adoration, and Brian felt a stab of envy. Not that he pined for the man's wife, but such honest love displayed for one and all to see was something Brian hoped to one day find in a woman he might call his own. Perhaps looking for a bride while he was here was not such a bad idea. His glance slid to Artemis.

"Lord Cherrington, I understand that you inherited your title recently due to the loss of your brother. Please accept our deepest sympathy," Lady Rothwell said with sincerity. He had to own that he liked the no-nonsense approach this lady displayed. She did not chase around a subject; she hit it straight on.

"Indeed," Rothwell chimed in.

"Again, I thank you," Brian shifted in his seat, slightly uncomfortable with this topic. Although he and Charles had never got on well, it stung that his brother had been cut down in the prime of his life. His feelings where Charles' death was concerned were too strong to discuss over dinner. Besides, he feared he would let his carefully controlled voice slip.

Artemis looked concerned. "I beg your pardon, Lord Cherrington, but what happened?"

"Charles' carriage was held up by the highwaymen, and he wound up getting himself killed."

Artemis went pale. "But I thought they had not harmed anyone."

He felt an odd urge to defend himself, or rather his alter ego. "The servants said it was an accident."

"Terrible situation, these highwaymen!" Rothwell snorted. "Robbing their betters. The *Morning Post* ran an editorial of several young ladies clamoring to be kissed by the scoundrels! As if any lady of sense would welcome such a thing! I'd give these fellows something they'd not soon forget if they dared attempt thievery against a Rothwell."

Brian caught the guilty glances exchanged between the ladies and knew they had not shared the news of their attack with the gentlemen. He wondered if her pink-tinted cheeks meant that Artemis was shamed by the memory of his kiss. She caught him looking at her, and he quickly looked away.

Again, Rothwell snorted. "They are cutthroats. I'm shamed that your brother, a fine man I am sure, met his end in such a way."

Brian wanted to change the conversation, but he did not wish to appear rude. " 'Tis a terrible thing."

"Those responsible are sure to be caught by the authorities," Lord Ashbourne said. "I understand some of the nobility are tired of waiting on Bow Street to bring these highwaymen to justice. I am surprised a reward for their capture has not been posted."

"Indeed," Brian said. He wanted to be the one that led to their capture. He had to own that he wanted the Leader to suffer by his own hand. "That would seem reasonable to expedite their demise."

"Let us hope they are caught soon," Lady Rothwell said with finality in order to close the subject.

Artemis pushed around the food on her plate. It

was ridiculous, she knew, but she had dreamed about the tall Highwayman nearly every night. He would no doubt be captured and thrown into Newgate, which is less than what he deserved for being party to the death of a peer. She was sorely ashamed of her silly dreams.

"Have you made your presentation at court?" Brian asked quietly.

Artemis had thought Lord Cherrington a coxcomb, but she was sorry for his loss. "Not yet. In two days, I make my bow."

"And your first social outing is when?"

"We attend a ball given by the Waterton-Smythes the evening after court," Artemis answered distractedly.

"I have the very same invitation on my desk. I shall reply with acceptance straight away."

Artemis nodded but did not answer. Even though she felt more charity toward him, she did not wish to encourage his suit. Clasby captured Lord Cherrington's attention, and she studied him more closely. He was an oddity to be sure. Dressed in flamboyant colors and high shirt points, he reminded her of a peacock. He was taller than her by several inches, but his wiry build and hawkish nose gave him a distinct birdlike quality that made Artemis want to laugh as she pictured him strutting about with feathers.

Clasby, Ashbourne, and even her father were treating him politely. But then, no matter how silly the man appeared to be, he was an earl.

After what seemed like an eternity, dinner concluded, and the ladies were excused to leave the gentlemen to their port. Once in the front drawing room, Miranda approached her with a lopsided grin.

"What do you think of our Lord Cherrington?" she asked.

Artemis rolled her eyes. "I am trying not to."

"Oh, come now," her stepmother chimed in. "He seems like a fine young fellow."

"Mama, he's a fop!" Artemis was aghast. "Did you not see Father's reaction to him?"

"His manners are nice," her stepmother said.

"Trust me," Artemis said with conviction. "Lord Cherrington is not what I want."

"Aha! So, you are not opposed to looking," Miranda mocked.

Artemis realized she had been bamboozled into a corner. "That is not what I meant."

"Then pray, enlighten us to your meaning," her stepmother teased.

"Lord Cherrington is simply not for me, he is too feminine by half. A man like that thinks only of his clothes."

Artemis would not mind meeting a gentleman she could favor. One who would not be put off by her plain looks and tall stature. A pair of blue eyes flashed before her mind. The Highwayman had not noticed her deficiencies. In fact, he had not laughed at her as the others did. But then, he had been preparing to disarm her. He might have treated her kindly, promised to return the ring, just to throw her off guard. After hearing how Lord Cherrington's brother had died, she vowed never again to think kindly of the tall Highwayman.

Chapter Three

$\mathcal{A}$rtemis stilled her fidgeting hands from outlining the stitching pattern on the Ashbourne carriage wall as she sat quietly while on the way to the opening ball of the Season. Besides her court appearance this morning, the Waterton-Smythe ball was her first *real* introduction to the *ton*. Her hair had been carefully arranged, her thick eyebrows had been painfully plucked, and her gown meticulously chosen.

The time had come to face the spiteful Waterton-Smythe sisters, the nastiest guests at the hunting party this past autumn. The two sisters had never been friendly toward her. She could only imagine what vicious gossip they might have spread about her breaking off her betrothal to Ashbourne.

She glanced up to find Ashbourne watching her. He gave her an encouraging nod that spoke volumes. He knew exactly what she worried over.

The carriage stopped in the circular drive, and Artemis waited until her father and Ashbourne had stepped out. She looked up at the vast townhouse, wishing the night to be over instead of just beginning.

"Chin up," Ashbourne whispered for her ears alone. "You've nothing to hang your head about."

Artemis tried to smile, but fear got the best of her. She wiped her hands unconsciously upon her skirt. She knew she had to face the disgrace of jilting Ashbourne. How she handled the situation this evening was bound to set the tone for her entire Season. She had to get it right; she had to act demure, as a lady should. She was not about to bring shame to the name of Rothwell in the lofty circles of Town by saying something out of turn.

As for Ashbourne and Miranda—one look at them and it was obvious that they were indeed meant for one another. They fared no damage from the events last November and had welcomed her as a dear friend.

Artemis lifted her chin and walked into the glittering ballroom. She stood stiffly, waiting nervously to be announced. Strains of music from the orchestra lilted through the night air filled with the scent of burning beeswax candles and various perfumes. Her knees felt weak, but she refused to succumb to the temptation to turn around and run. A Rothwell did not flinch in the face of a challenge!

Brian saw Artemis Rothwell standing at the top of the stairs. She commanded attention not only because of her height but by the way she carried herself, her head held high with almost regal deportment. He liked that. She was certainly no shrinking violet.

She was not what society would call a beauty. Although, she could not claim classic features, Brian found her extremely attractive. She wore a white gown as expected at her first come-out, but the very lack of ribbons and ruffles made the dress unique. It draped her body like a second skin, falling softly past her generous hips. She appeared every inch for whom she was named, Artemis—Greek goddess of the hunt.

He nearly laughed aloud at his fanciful thoughts. He had been paying very close attention to the dandy set of men's clothes, even if he did choose outlandish combinations. But he had an eye for feminine fashion as well. He knew what looked good on a woman.

He popped a small puff pastry into his mouth as he watched Artemis descend the stairs after her name and that of her family and friends were announced.

"Scandalous," Miss Waterton-Smythe whispered as she came up to stand beside him. "Artemis Rothwell, brought out by the very woman who stole her intended."

Brian nearly choked on another puff. "La, but surely, you jest, *ma chérie*."

"No, I do not. My dear Lord Cherrington, have you not heard?"

He knew the pinched-nose miss would no doubt enlighten him. "I have not." He shifted his weight and raised his quizzing glass to inspect Miss Waterton-Smythe's expression of superiority.

"Miss Rothwell was betrothed to Lord Ashbourne this past autumn. After her proud papa announced it, Miss Rothwell suddenly jilted him and Lord Ashbourne became engaged to Lady Crandle, now Lady Ashbourne. It's been said that Lord and Lady Ashbourne were once in love years ago."

Brian feigned the right amount of shock. It was indeed a story he hoped to hear from Miss Rothwell's point of view. "My goodness." Turning the quizzing glass upon the couple in question, he added. "Pon rep, but it appears the right choice has been made."

Miss Waterton-Smythe did not agree. "I have it straight from Princess Lieven that Miss Rothwell might not receive vouchers this year. One simply cannot jilt a peer without consequences."

Brian tsk'd as he should, but he did not care for either of the mean-spirited Waterton-Smythe sisters. He did not know which one he spoke to at the moment, but it mattered not. Both were after him. He had an old title and wealth, each a prerequisite for the lofty sticklers that hosted this evening's grand event. "For shame," he clucked as he jotted his name down upon the dance card Miss Waterton-Smythe dangled in front of his nose. "Had I been Miss Rothwell's intended, I would not have let her get away."

"Indeed," Miss Waterton-Smythe said with an affronted smile before floating along toward another gentleman of means.

Brian smiled with amusement then looked around to find where Artemis had gone. He spotted her standing near a pretty young lady, and the two were talking with animation as if they had not seen each other for some time. He felt the corners of his mouth lift, and he made his way toward them.

When he reached the two, he bowed with great decorum and an expertly extended leg. "Ladies," he purred, quizzing glass poised for perusal. "You are both divine visions this evening."

The pretty one blushed furiously, and a giggle escaped her bow-shaped lips.

"Good evening, Lord Cherrington," Artemis said with almost bored resignation.

"I thought you would have been glad to see me." He acted hurt by her indifference. "Who is your exquisite friend?"

Artemis narrowed her eyes as if trying to figure out his game. He smiled innocently and waited.

Artemis started cautiously. "Lord Cherrington, may I present Miss Harriet Whitlow."

Brian bowed low over the girl's hand, depositing a quick kiss upon her knuckles. "Charmed, my dear Miss Whitlow."

Again, a deep pink flushed the girl's cheeks. "Pleased to meet you," she said.

"Now then," Brian said. "Do you perhaps have a dance card with an empty space begging for my name?"

Miss Whitlow held it out for him to inspect.

Brian scrawled his name along with many others on a vacant line next to a cotillion. "Your servant, Miss Whitlow." He turned toward Artemis. "And yours, Miss Rothwell?"

Artemis hesitated as if she could not decide to a dance with him, but in the end she produced her card. It was quite empty, but then she had only just arrived. He scratched his name in two places, one of them—a waltz.

She read her card and said, "I have not gained permission to waltz."

"No matter," Brian said. "We can promenade

about the room, then. Ladies, I must bid you adieu, as there are other cards to be signed and so little time." He bent to take hold of Artemis' hand, but she kept it firmly behind her back. Instead, he bowed low with a flourish of his hand. He winked at her, then left in search of ladies to woo with hopes of gleaning information about the other gentlemen present.

"That is the new Lord Cherrington?" Harriet asked with a grin.

"It is. Did you know his brother?" Artemis asked.

"I met him only once. He was indeed shorter and quite handsome, but the gossips often remarked that he was wild and irresponsible. He consorted with the demimonde."

"Really?" she asked with surprise. "Lord Cherrington hardly appears to walk in his brother's footsteps."

"There is an odd bit of charm about him, do you not think?"

"Harriet, he is a popinjay!" Artemis twirled her dance card about her finger.

"Yes, but did you not see the twinkle in his gorgeous blue eyes? I think he favors you, dear."

"Please," Artemis groaned. "Do not remind me." She had not even noticed the color of his eyes. She squinted too hard at the blindingly bright canary yellow waistcoat he wore.

"Very well. Let us talk of something else. It has been an age since I saw you last. You must bring me up to date since your last letter."

"Well, many things really, but, oh, the music is

starting, and I think the gentleman approaching is your partner," Artemis said.

"You are correct. Let us meet then tomorrow morning, shall we say nine o'clock at Hyde Park for a ride?"

Artemis nodded with pleasure. She had not ridden since she had arrived, and she sorely missed it. "Nine o'clock."

"What happens then, do you turn into a pumpkin?"

The cool male voice gave her a start. Artemis turned around to find Lord Ranton standing closer than comfort allowed. "Lord Ranton."

"I bid you good evening, Miss Rothwell. Welcome to London."

Despite the fact that she had overheard him insult her at a country ball over four months ago, she still admired the man's good looks. He was not as tall as she, but he was well built with wavy dark brown hair that cried out to be touched. She found her voice. "Thank you, Lord Ranton. Did you enjoy your Christmas?" She could have kicked herself for asking such a lame question. She sounded like a country bumpkin, indeed.

He smiled. "Indeed I did. And you?"

"Very much." She fell silent, unsure of herself.

Lord Ranton looked bored, but he remained next to her. " 'Tis quite a change from the assembly rooms at Shepeshead, is it not?" His voice held a hint of sarcastic condensation.

"Yes." She felt nervous. Why had he approached her? Did he wish to make a mockery of her yet again?

"Might I add my name to your dance card?" he asked. "Unless it is already full."

She handed him her card without a word. She could not afford to offend anyone, least of all a friend of her hostesses.

"Ah, I see Lord Cherrington has claimed two dances. You must know him well. I have never seen him before in Town."

"He's been abroad," Artemis answered, remembering the conversation at dinner the night he had joined them. Her defenses rose, ready to defend him. "His brother was killed by the highwaymen, and he came home to take his place."

"I see." Lord Ranton returned her card. "Until the next quadrille, then." He made a slight bow and left.

Artemis tried to breathe normally, but could not. Lord Ranton had scribbled his name for two dances!

"Was that Lord Ranton?" Mr. Clasby stood before her.

"Yes."

"What did he want?"

"Two dances." Artemis hoped Lord Ranton looked at her differently. She had worked hard to improve herself since their last meeting.

"Might I have a dance?"

"Of course." Artemis distractedly handed Mr. Clasby her card. She was watching Lord Ranton as he made his way toward other ladies, marking his name upon their cards.

"Ah, right," Mr. Clasby coughed. "Have you seen Ashbourne?"

"Somewhere." Artemis gestured toward the refreshment table.

"There are many gentlemen here, Artemis. Keep

your wits about you. This is merely the calm before the storm of dance partners you will soon have."

That statement brought her back to earth. "What do you mean, Mr. Clasby?"

He gave her an encouraging smile. "Only that you can do much better than Lord Ranton. I will be back for the next dance, since Cherrington has this one."

Artemis felt her cheeks heat. The music ended and Harriet's partner deposited her next to Artemis, thus giving her a needed escape from having to respond to Mr. Clasby's well-meaning advice.

Harriet smiled at him "Mr. Clasby, how nice to see you again."

"Miss Whitlow."

Artemis did not have the chance to join in their conversation, since Lord Cherrington appeared to claim her hand. She kept looking back at Harriet and Mr. Clasby, wondering what they said. Harriet looked serious indeed.

"Anything amiss?" Lord Cherrington escorted her to the dance floor.

"Nothing."

"You look distressed."

"But I am not," Artemis nearly snapped.

"Very well. Tell me about the dark-haired gentleman who spoke to you."

"Mr. Clasby?" Other dancers formed sets around them.

"*Non, ma chérie*. The other man."

"Lord Ranton?"

"*Oui*."

Why was it so important with whom she spoke? "I do not know him well." They joined a set.

"Ah, then he too was lured by your beauty."

That falsehood sparked her anger. "There is no need to mock me, Lord Cherrington. I know perfectly well that I am no beauty."

The music started. They bowed to one another and then the others in their set.

"I do not mock, my dove," he said with an intensity that gave her pause.

She stared at him and had to agree with her friend, his eyes were a lovely shade of bright blue.

They touched hands and circled to the beat but remained quiet the rest of the dance, leaving Artemis to wonder about him. He moved with fluid grace, his gaze never straying far from her. She did not feel like a giant with him, since he was a good bit taller than she. She rather liked looking up to her dance partner.

There was something else about him that eluded definition. For once in her life, she felt rather feminine, which was absurd when one considered Lord Cherrington's effeminate manners. The dance ended before she could refine too much upon it. Lord Cherrington left her near Harriet and promised to return for their *waltz*.

"Lord Cherrington is a superb dancer," Harriet said after he took his leave. "And he is making quite a stir."

"Of course he is, just look at him," Artemis said.

"That's not what I mean. Everyone thinks he is quite amusing, especially the ladies."

"One cannot help but be amused when faced with a gentleman peacock!"

Harriet giggled. "Oh, that is not fair."

"But true." Artemis turned serious. "Whatever were you and Mr. Clasby so serious about when I left?"

"Mr. Clasby has asked that I help you this Season, where the gentlemen are concerned at least. Lord Ranton, though socially acceptable, is not the most desirable *parti*. He has a habit of seeking out ladies of substantial means. His father had a terrible habit of gambling too deep, leaving Ranton quite with pockets to let."

Artemis suspected as much, but still she suffered a slight pang of regret. She was fooling herself if she believed any man would want her for her looks. She was sadly lacking in that quarter. She had a sizable dowry that Artemis knew was a powerful attraction for many a gentleman in London. She did indeed have to keep her wits. Any fellow who paid her a bit of attention was most likely thinking with his empty purse.

When she remained quiet, Harriet pursed her lips. "Please forgive me for my harshness, but I do not wish your feelings to be hurt again by that man."

"Of course." Artemis patted her friend's hand. "I truly appreciate your concern. You have already experienced a Season. I would be indeed wise to seek your counsel." She trusted Harriet's judgment.

Harriet sighed, but said nothing more.

Over the course of the next few dances, several gentlemen signed Artemis' dance card. Fate had not determined her to be a wallflower and for that she was grateful. She held her head high, even though she towered over the tiny women upon the dance floor and stood taller than most of the gentlemen as well.

When she finally stood alone, she noticed Lord Cherrington with several young ladies who hung on his every word. The Waterton-Smythe sisters did not appear pleased with this development, and Artemis nearly laughed when she realized that the sisters had hopes of ensnaring the well-to-do lord peacock for themselves.

"You look amused." Lord Ranton held out his hand for their second dance.

"Lord Cherrington is popular," Artemis said with forced indifference.

"Indeed. He's a different sort of fellow."

"He is that."

Lord Ranton appeared most congenial, so she relaxed. Perhaps, he had not truly meant the coarse words she had overheard him utter to one of the Waterton-Smythe sisters last autumn. Perhaps, he no longer thought she looked like a horse.

Lord Ranton led her in a fast quadrille. They had little time or breath to speak, and quickly Artemis forgot that she was so much taller than everyone else in her set. She laughed with pure enjoyment as the dance progressed, and she moved through the steps with near grace. And then it happened.

One minute she was twirling and the next she tripped, falling to her knees upon the floor.

"My dear Miss Rothwell," Lord Ranton blustered. "Let me help you. I beg your pardon, I faltered. Considering your stature, it must have been a long fall."

Her face ignited with embarrassment. She did not

know how to interpret Lord Ranton's remark. He smiled kindly enough, yet his words were double-edged and they cut her to the quick.

She took his hand, however, not wishing to make more of a spectacle. Ladies tittered behind their fans, and gentlemen tried to hide their guffaws. Lord Cherrington, her partner to sit out from the waltz, was soon at her side, giving Lord Ranton a sour look.

"I am indeed fine, Lord Ranton. And, yes, it was a long way down." She managed a brilliant smile, which earned her approving nods from the other couples in their interrupted set.

"So glad that you have retained your good humor." Lord Ranton turned to Lord Cherrington. "And I see that I leave you in good hands. I fear our set cannot regain the finale of the dance." Lord Ranton bowed and took his leave.

"Good riddance," Lord Cherrington uttered under his breath.

But she had heard. "What was that?"

"The lummox is a clumsy ox. 'Twas his own two left feet that caused your fall."

"Lord Cherrington, really. Perhaps the fault was my own. Besides, I can be clumsy. It was merely an accident."

The strains of a waltz began, and Lord Cherrington suddenly pulled her into his arms. "Perhaps you simply have not had the right partner, *ma chérie*."

"My lord!" Artemis sputtered. "I have not yet been given permission. Let me go at once!"

"Trust me," he whispered. "And do call me Cherry." He actually winked at her.

Artemis gasped irritably. She would do no such

thing! She tried to pull away, but Lord Cherrington was surprisingly strong for a bribble. She was whisked into the center of the dance floor by his wiry strength and in no time they moved as one.

"You see?" He gave her a cheeky grin. "I told you."

Artemis rolled her eyes. He was an excellent dancer. He led her easily, making her own steps sure. "You told me that you are light on your feet? That is quite obvious."

"*Touché*, my Amazon vixen."

"I am not your *anything*, Lord Cherrington."

"Perhaps not yet, but give it time." His merry blue eyes were looking decidedly wicked. "I am the best dance partner for you. *Non?*"

"Only in that for once someone is taller than me."

"We fit rather nicely."

Artemis experienced an odd shiver at his bold flirtation. She hoped he did not land her in the suds. It was bad enough that she waltzed before she had gained permission, but she had not even received approval for vouchers to Almack's! Miranda and her stepmother were bound to lecture her for committing such a gross affront to the rules of her come-out.

Swirling across the floor and weaving in and out, they rounded the outside edge of the other couples dancing. Artemis had just started to enjoy the sensation of waltzing, when she glimpsed Lady Jersey speaking to Miranda in a most disapproving manner. Her heart sank to the bottom of her slippers. She had made a terrible introduction to society. Falling down in a quadrille and now this! It was Lord Cherrington's fault.

"Look at what you have done. Lady Jersey is scolding Lady Ashbourne for my behavior."

He only winked and whispered, "Trust me."

Brian held on tightly to Artemis' hand once the waltz ended. He did not want her darting off before he could make reparations with Lady Jersey, the most highly regarded of the sticklers. Brian had met Lady Jersey before. Her mother, Lady Frances, was in fact a friend of his mother's. He could make things right. Lady Jersey had been fond of both his brother and himself since they were mere lads.

He walked toward the arbiter of society, talking to Lady Ashbourne. Artemis pulled at his hand as if to bolt. "Do be still," he hissed.

"You are going to ruin me even more, before I have even had the chance to redeem myself."

"Whatever are you talking about? You are far from ruined."

"Surely you have heard about my brief engagement to Lord Ashbourne. I am not stupid. The Waterton-Smythe sisters have been spreading it about all night."

He slowed his pace and looked closely at her. "So? You made a mistake, and it was before you had a Season. The Waterton-Smythes are simply trying to knock you out of the running."

Artemis snorted.

" 'Tis true. You are a valuable young lady, Miss Rothwell."

"So I have been told."

The hard glint in her eyes told Brian that she was not happy about it. In fact, she did not act like the typical young woman on the market for a husband.

She did not flirt or cast her eyes about in flutters. She looked a man straight in the eye as if she counted him an equal. So far, nothing about Artemis Rothwell could be labeled as commonplace.

"Ah, Lady Jersey." Brian bowed low, capturing her hand for a brief kiss.

At her expression of confusion, Lady Ashbourne stepped in. "Lord Cherrington, how lovely to see you. I fear Miss Rothwell—"

"Brian?" Lady Jersey cut her off. Surprise gave way to recognition. "My goodness, man, what have you done to yourself!"

"I have been traveling abroad," Brian said with his quizzing glass raised. He bowed again, for good measure.

"But I thought your mama said you were in . . ."

"The Continent, India, a rather long *Grand Tour*," Brian supplied with a Gallic shrug.

She still looked confused, as if his mother had told her something completely different, but she shrugged it off. "It has been years, my dear, years. My goodness how you have changed."

Brian noticed that both Miss Rothwell and Lady Ashbourne watched him intently. He had impressed them with his own connection to high society. Frankly, he had forgot about Lady Jersey, until tonight. He summoned his sweetest smile and cleared his throat.

"Lady Jersey," he began, "please do not judge Miss Rothwell severely for waltzing without permission. 'Tis my doing, in order to demonstrate how divinely she moves with grace and agility."

That earned him a smile from Lady Ashbourne and

a raised eyebrow from Lady Jersey. He did not dare look at Artemis. Her hand remained in his, but he could sense the tension in her.

Lady Jersey gave Artemis a tender smile of encouragement before saying, "I saw you fall, child. A most uncomfortable situation."

"Indeed." Artemis nodded.

Then Lady Jersey skewered him with her direct gaze. "And you sought to play knight-errant and whisk the dear girl into a waltz to do what pray tell? Cause more of a stir, since it is the girl's first bow in society and everyone knows she has not been given permission to waltz?"

"I figured it would take their minds off the mere stumble," he said with a flourish of his hand.

Lady Jersey pursed her twitching lips before giving over to genuine laughter. "Oh, that is rich indeed." Then with a nod to Artemis, Lady Jersey gave her blessing. "You are indeed granted permission to waltz, my dear, which you performed admirably." Then she turned to Lady Ashbourne. "And, Miranda, I shall approve those vouchers to Almack's. I look forward to seeing more of Miss Rothwell this Season."

They were dismissed, as Lady Jersey, the grand Queen of Society, moved through her court.

"Lord Cherrington, how can I ever thank you!" Lady Ashbourne breathed with relief.

"By allowing me to call upon Miss Rothwell."

"Why, of course you may." Lady Ashbourne darted a glance at Artemis and so did Brian.

The young lady the fuss was over, stood quietly with her chin raised in defiance.

Chapter Four

*A*rtemis stretched her arms high over her head after she got out of bed. She had slept deeply, considering the previous day and evening had been wrought with nerves and emotions such as embarrassment, frustration, and a host of other things a person loathes to feel.

She ambled to her desk, where her chocolate had been placed along with the latest copy of the *Morning Post*. Picking up a steaming cup and the newspaper, she settled into an overstuffed chair in front of the fireplace that had been stoked to a cheery crackle. She took a sip and fingered through the *Post*.

No current news of the highwaymen, or any notices of the Rothwell ring. She and her stepmother had left instructions with several pawnbrokers to discreetly advertise if they came upon the ring. Her stepmother said she would pay whatever necessary to get it back.

Artemis stopped at the society news when she spotted something familiar. Lord Cherrington was referenced, and Artemis shamefully realized that she was noted as well. Her face blazed as she read the column again.

> *A certain Cherry made the sourest of grapes appear sweet to Lady J last evening at the W-S ball. So sweet did the young lady appear to our ruling arbiter, that she was given a nod to waltz even after completing said dance.*

"Sour grapes, indeed," Artemis muttered. She threw the paper down, got up and walked to the window that overlooked the back courtyard. She owed a great deal of thanks to Lord Cherrington for smoothing her path, but to be so described in a public newspaper was distasteful in the extreme. To add insult to the embarrassing injury to her pride, Lord Cherrington had made it quite clear that he wished to court her. And Miranda approved!

"You, sir, are a silly dandy merely playing games," she said aloud as she stared out of her window.

Harriet Whitlow had filled Artemis in completely regarding the gossip surrounding Lord Cherrington. He had good lineage, with the title of an earl. He was wealthy with no need to line his already plump pockets with the Rothwell dowry. Harriet had said that many of the ladies adored him already because they spoke the same language of frills and fashion. The men were wary, but overall accepting.

"Of course, the ladies fawn over him. Lord Cherrington not only engages in talk of clothes and trinkets, he actually enjoys such empty conversations!" Artemis argued with her own thoughts. She shook her head. She was acting like a fool, talking to herself.

A streak of white in the yard beyond Miranda's back courtyard caught her attention. She narrowed her gaze, hoping to see it again, and nearly fell down when she did. A tall man dressed only in buff pantaloons and a white shirt practiced with a sword out-of-doors.

Due to the man's height and slender build, she wondered if it might be Lord Cherrington. Miranda had said that his townhouse was close by. Artemis watched with awe at the grace of movement the tall man displayed. He parried and thrust with confidence against a man of shorter stature who retaliated with quick jabs and almost jerky sidesteps in comparison to the tall man's fluid motion. Was this man Lord Cherrington?

The clock in her room struck half past eight, and Artemis pulled herself away from the window. She had promised to meet Harriet in Hyde Park at nine o'clock.

Artemis urged her mare toward Rotten Row, the sandy track in Hyde Park, where she was supposed to meet Harriet. She was late. It was already ten minutes past the hour of nine.

"Good morning," Artemis called to the female rider atop a dapple-gray mount.

"I thought perhaps you had forgotten." Harriet waved in return.

"To ride?" Artemis brought her mare next to Harriet's gelding. "Never."

Harriet laughed. "How are you this fine spring morning? Did you see the *Post*?"

"Of course. It is beside mentioning."

"Actually, Artie, 'tis not so bad. You have been given a nod of acceptance from Lady Jersey. Your Season is set, and everyone knows it."

Artemis tipped her head. "What do you mean?"

"The Waterton-Smythe sisters will be mold-green with envy. No matter how hard they tried to stir up trouble about you jilting Ashbourne, you have gained vouchers to Almack's and permission to waltz on the same night of your entrance into society. There is nothing the Waterton-Smythes can do to you now. You are quite considered *good ton*!"

It was Artemis' turn to laugh. "Really?" She owed Lord Cherrington more than mere gratitude.

"Yes, really." A gleam sparkled in her friend's eyes. "We did not have much time to chat last night, and you must tell me the latest on the whereabouts of your stepmother's ring." Artemis had quietly shared the whole story with Harriet over tea before their bows at court.

"None at all. None of the pawnbrokers have seen it. I do believe the highwaymen still have it. Did you know it is being said that the bandits might be gentlemen?"

Harriet giggled. "Of course I have heard that. Why do you think so many ladies are staging carriage accidents for a kiss?"

Artemis made a face. Her thoughts whirled. "There has to be a way to get that ring back."

"Did you go to the Bow Street Runners?"

"No. I cannot until my parents return to Rothwell

Park. My father would no doubt find out, and that we cannot have." Artemis tapped the end of her riding crop against her lips. "There must be a way to find out who these men are if they are indeed gentlemen, do you not think?"

Harriet looked shocked. "My goodness, Artie, that could be dangerous. Besides, how would you go about it?"

"I do not know. But I will think of something."

"Good morning, ladies." Lord Cherrington, dressed to the height of garish fashion, reigned in his horse next to them.

"Lord Cherrington, please tell Artemis that it would be sheer folly to attempt to discover who the highwaymen might be," Harriet said quickly.

Artemis cast her a sharp look, but to no avail. Harriet smiled sweetly. Lord Cherrington actually paled beneath the powder he wore.

"Whatever can you be thinking, Miss Rothwell?" His voice was so shrill that it nearly hurt her ears.

"Miss Whitlow exaggerates," Artemis said calmly. "I simply wish to have a ring of extreme importance to my family returned."

"Do not say that you were attacked?" He looked shocked.

"We were, but please do not breathe a word of it. My father cannot know, else he is bound to go after the cutthroats himself and send me packing besides. No one was harmed, and nothing else was taken, only the ring."

He rubbed his chin. "Very well, I shall remain silent, but for that I ask a favor in return."

Artemis held her breath. She feared to speculate.

She cast a quick glance at Harriet, who appeared considerably amused by the whole interaction. "What is it that you wish, Lord Cherrington?"

"This may be an ongoing favor, as the only thing I can think of is to ask that you reserve a waltz for me at Almack's."

"What do you mean, ongoing favor?"

"Only that I might think of other things in future."

Artemis gasped with indignation. "Sir, that is blackmail."

Lord Cherrington grinned so broadly that he appeared very like a rooster who had just taken the choicest grains. "That is the price for my silence."

Artemis turned to Harriet for help.

"Do not look at me, Artie." Harriet started to giggle.

"Harriet you are absolutely no help at all. And a pox on you for enjoying this."

Lord Cherrington, however, looked taken aback by her vulgar language, but she did not care. If he wished to be around her, then he would see the real Artemis Rothwell!

"Come, Artie, let us do what we came here for and ride," Harriet said. "Lord Cherrington, do join us."

"Miss Whitlow, I intend to."

Artemis made a face, forgetting all about the debt of gratitude she owed the man for salvaging her dignity and placing her firmly in an acceptable position within the *ton*. "Very well, Cherry," she said with a saucy grin. He had asked her to call him thus, so be it. "Let us see if you can keep up." With a kick of her heels, she and her mare sped off down the sandy track.

Brian did not waste a moment. He urged his mount forward, but held back from an all out gallop, in order to watch Miss Rothwell's excellent form. She was born to a saddle, and he expected nothing less from her. She was the most original woman he had ever met. She was nothing like the shrinking violets that were officer's daughters in India. All of them, pampered misses who did not dare tarnish their pert little noses in the mid-afternoon sun. Nor was she like the grasping ladies of London, looking for wealth or a title or fame as the latest Incomparable.

Artie Rothwell, how the nickname suited her, was the woman for him, he was sure of it. By all that was Holy, he would have to keep his eye on her if what Miss Whitlow said was in fact true. Artie had no business trying to cross the Leader.

He'd do what he could to keep her out of harm's way, which would no doubt put a kink into his own search for the identities of the highwaymen. Or perhaps, he should play along with her idea and see if two heads searching might prove to be better than one. Either way, he would keep her safe.

Thank goodness he had made it on time! Brian entered the hallowed halls of Almack's. He had heard tales of the doors being closed promptly at eleven o'clock, and not even the Duke of Wellington was allowed to enter late.

He had been on another robbery this afternoon. Just about the time he had hoped to call on Artemis at the Ashbourne townhouse. Thank goodness, Clancy had stopped off at *John Fellows'* flat in Cheapside to deliver clothes Brian had forgotten to leave there earlier that morning. A note had been left under the door. The time he would be picked up by a hired hack was scrawled on a poorly made piece of parchment. It was short notice, but that was how the Leader worked. He kept them continually off balance, with no forewarning, and no way to prepare or follow.

After dividing the loot between them, Brian finally made it back to Town in time to wash, change, and dash off to Almack's in order to claim his promised waltz from Artemis Rothwell.

Making his way through the throng of people attending the opening night of the assembly rooms, Brian looked about for his tall Amazon. She was determined not to like him, but he was as determined to reverse that, even though he had to play the fribble.

He spotted her next to two gentlemen who were quite interested in what his Amazon said. He felt an odd rush of something very near to jealousy, and he nearly laughed. He had never been jealous over a woman in his life. He had always been jealous of his ne'er-do-well brother, who owned an unshakable place of honor in their father's eyes, but that was entirely different from wanting to knock the block off of some bloke for listening too intently to the woman he intended to win over.

Brian pulled an intricately carved snuffbox from his waistcoat pocket and pinched a bit of snuff. He inhaled quickly then sneezed. Wiping his nose delicately with a scented handkerchief, he was ready to play his part.

Artemis saw the peacock making his way toward

her out of the corner of her eye. Lord Cherrington looked stern, if such a thing was possible. He minced his way toward them, his nose twitching.

"And what does your father have to say on the matter, Miss Rothwell?"

Oh, drat! She had missed Lord Cole's question. "I beg your pardon, my lord, but I did not hear you."

"Cross-breeding," Lord Cole said. "How does your father feel about crossing breeds with his hunters?"

"He has had great success. Castlestone, my father's finest stallion is a cross of a thoroughbred and an ancient Irish hunting breed. I believe that if you stud too narrow within one breed, you result with a weaker steed."

"Well said Miss Rothwell. I am not surprised that you know so much about horseflesh after witnessing your prowess in the saddle today." Lord Cherrington bowed to both gentlemen after lowering his quizzing glass. He offered his greetings and introduction.

"Thank you," she said.

The other gentleman, Mr. Mellowby, asked, "A good rider is she?"

"Indeed she is." Lord Cherrington nodded. "But, alas, gentlemen, I have been promised a waltz with Miss Rothwell and have come to claim her, as I believe it shall be the next dance."

Lord Cole excused himself, but Mr. Mellowby hesitated before he finally said, "I shall see you later, my dear."

"How do you know the next dance is a waltz, Lord Cherrington?" Artemis asked.

"A mere guess, but it had the desired effect."

Again, he raised his quizzing glass. "Look, your suitors are gone."

"They were not suitors," Artemis said. "We were merely speaking of the hunters my father breeds."

"Ah, well, even so. Mr. Mellowby, I feel compelled to warn you, is an outright fortune hunter."

Artemis narrowed her eyes. "How do you know?"

"I hear things at my club, I assure you. Lord Cole is a respectable Irish peer, but are you quite certain you wish to live amongst those roughshod brigands for part of the year?"

Artemis was speechless for only a moment. "Lord Cherrington, I have no intention of entertaining thoughts of either man for your information. I have no desire to *lure* any man into parson's mousetrap."

He looked her up and down with his infuriating quizzing glass. "And yet you could easily succeed with perhaps a little more confidence and a few different gowns. I rather liked the one you wore at the Waterton-Smythe's. And do call me Cherry."

Was the man serious? He had looked her over not as a man typically would, but as a dressmaker might, and she found herself curious. She thought the white muslin she wore adequate. It resembled the other dresses worn by girls making their fist bow. Could she actually learn something from this ridiculously feminine man?

"If not for a husband, why have you come to London for a Season?" He held out his arm as the strains of a waltz did indeed float in the air.

"To see the sights, go to Astley's Royal Amphitheatre, experience an ice at Gunter's, and visit the museums. That sort of thing."

"And have you done those things?"

Artemis wrinkled her nose. "No." There had been no time when she arrived, what with the flurry of fittings, and the lessons and preparations for making her curtsy at court. "Why have you come to London?" She changed the focus to him.

"To meet with the Cherrington solicitors now that I am the earl and, of course, to find a bride." He gave her a wink.

"Truly?" She nearly laughed.

"Indeed there are several I have my eye upon."

"I see. Perhaps you would care to tell who they are?" Artemis asked, curious.

"I am not quite ready to discuss the matter as of yet, but rest assured when I have made my choice, you will be the first to know." He gave her another mischievous wink.

"Very well. I can only assume that I am not on your list, since you did not call upon me this afternoon."

"Missed me, did you?"

"Not quite. But Miranda remarked upon it. I fear I did not properly thank you for your arbitration on my behalf with Lady Jersey."

Lord Cherrington waved his perfumed hand in dismissal, and then pulled her into his embrace for the waltz. "Think nothing of it. Did you have many callers?"

"A few."

"Anyone I know?"

"I do not know. Lord Cole was there. He likes to talk of horses, as you might already have guessed.

Mr. Mellowby, Lord Ranton, and a few other gentlemen that I cannot remember their names."

"Ah." He dipped her slightly to avoid another couple.

They were quiet for a few moments, and Artemis let herself follow Lord Cherrington's excellent lead. Although he was an odd fellow, he was confident upon the dance floor. She felt comfortable with him, if it could be called that. His hand upon her back was firm yet light, and he held her hand gently.

Warmth radiated from his palm to hers with none of the sticky dampness that Mr. Mellowby had displayed when they danced to a quadrille. Lord Cherrington moved effortlessly with grace, and a vision of the man with the sword from this morning came to mind.

"Lord Cherrington, do you fence?"

He looked surprised and then nodded. "Yes, I do. In fact, I practice often."

"Out-of-doors in your courtyard?"

"Yes. Why?"

"Because, I believe I saw you this morning while you were at practice. I was wondering if perhaps I might ask you for an ongoing favor of my own."

"Of course, I am your willing servant." He inclined his head with a bow.

Artemis chewed her bottom lip. She knew what she was about to ask was not at all the thing. In fact, it might be considered beyond the pale, but since they were neighbors, there was no reason she could not slip out before her morning chocolate was served. No one need ever know. He had protected her reputation with Lady Jersey. She did not believe that he would do anything to ruin her or set her up for ridicule. And she needed to learn to defend herself, if it came to that, while trying to get the Rothwell ring back.

"Miss Rothwell, you have a favor?" He cocked one eyebrow.

She shook herself out of woolgathering and asked, "Would you teach me how to wield a sword?"

Good and merciful God! Brian swallowed his shock, but he faltered in his dance steps. "I beg your pardon?"

"I know it is not exactly a request one might receive from a lady," she explained. "But I must learn and after seeing your expertise this morning, I knew I had to ask."

"How did you happen to see me?" He had to be careful what image he portrayed in his own courtyard from now on!

"My window overlooks your courtyard."

They swayed to the music and dipped and turned, and he conveniently moved them slightly away from the other dancers toward the outer corner of the floor. "And why must you learn?" He pulled her closer so they could speak softly.

"I am proficient with a pistol, even better with arrows and bow, but I have never learned to use a sword."

He chuckled. He knew exactly how well the girl held a pistol. That vision had been burned into his memory forever. "You still have not answered the why."

"My own personal reasons," she said.

"And what if I refuse, *ma chérie*?"

"I will find something to hold over your head, just as you have to me."

"Hmmmm. I certainly do not wish that, as no doubt you would deliver upon your threat. Perhaps, you might tell me how you managed to jilt Lord Ashbourne and end up sponsored by his lady wife all within the space of less than six months? For that tale, I will teach you the sport of fencing."

He watched her consider his offer and was pleased when she agreed with a hearty, "Done.

"But not here," she whispered. "Our waltz is coming to a close, and it is rather a long story. I shall explain all tomorrow morning, at what time pray?"

"Seven o'clock," Brian whispered. He had nothing to lose. If they were found out, he'd offer for Artemis Rothwell right there and then. It mattered not. He had to marry eventually, and there was no female he liked better. But even more so, he would have the chance to get to know her. This would give him the perfect opportunity to spend time in her company as well as keep a close eye upon her activities.

The music ended, and Brian noted that Lord Ranton hung about as if he planned to approach Artemis once they left the dance floor. "Your friend is here," he said.

Artemis turned and saw Lord Ranton walking toward them. "He is not really a friend."

"A suitor, then, since he did call upon you this afternoon."

"I honestly do not know how to interpret the attentions of Lord Ranton," she said quietly. "Besides, he came very early and stayed only the briefest of moments. Hardly the actions of a beau."

Brian leaned near her ear. "Try not to fall, my dove, else I will be obliged to save that tantalizing bottom of yours."

Artemis felt her eyes go wide. She turned to give Lord Cherrington the set-down he deserved after such a remark, but the confounded man gingerly addressed Lord Ranton, so there was nothing to be done. How she looked forward to sparring with him on the morrow, but at the other end of a sword.

Chapter Five

A quarter hour before seven o'clock, Artemis peeked out of her window to see if he was there. He was! She took a deep breath and finished lacing up her half boots. She dressed as simply as she could, in a plain wool gown that buttoned up to her neck. She wore no stays, simply a cotton chemise underneath. She hoped this would do.

Before leaving her room, she looked about her bedchamber. She had plumped the pillows under the covers so that it looked like someone still slept there. It would have to fool the maid who brought her chocolate every morning near nine o'clock. If it did not, she would no doubt hear the commotion while at Lord Cherrington's.

She quietly made her way down the stairs, a thrill of excitement sluicing through her with every step. She exited through a convenient side door that led to the small kitchen garden as quietly as she could. Some of the servants were bustling about, and she hoped none of them noticed her. She dashed across the lawn into Lord Cherrington's courtyard.

"Good morning, Cherry," she said breathlessly.

He turned and smiled, his eyes looking danger-ously dark for a fop. But he did not look quite like the Town dandy this morning. Dressed in plain buff pantaloons tucked into polished boots and a white lawn shirt with a collar of respectable height, com-plete with a perfectly tied cravat, he looked more like a country gentleman than a man of fashion. And then she saw his face. The appealing picture he made was diminished with his usual face powder, making his skin look terribly pale.

She sighed.

"Good morning, Artie," he said. "Might I call you thus, since we are to be fencing partners?"

Artemis tipped her head in agreement. "Of course. When do we start?"

"This minute. Come and I will test which blade best fits your hand."

Artemis followed him to a table with a large heavy cloth laid out upon it. Several swords and smaller knifes were laying neatly in a row. Her eyes wid-ened. "You have so many."

" 'Tis a hobby of mine, really. I have always de-sired to remain active, and since I am no fan of Gen-tleman Jackson's, nor do I care for hunting, I use this to keep me fit."

Fit? Artemis doubted there could ever be found a measure of fat upon the man. He was naturally thin. "You do not foxhunt?"

"It has never been to my taste. I suppose my sym-pathy for the fox runs too deep."

"What of other hunts, grouse or partridge?" Ar-temis asked.

Cherry shook his head. "I would much rather shoot targets."

"Oh." Hearing that he had no interest in hunting disappointed her, but she shrugged it off. It did not matter. She doubted she would see him again after this Season. Lord Cherrington could not be counted a desirable suitor; her father would never accept such a man. But perhaps, she might call him friend.

She ran her fingers along the shiny blades of steel. Cool to the touch, she shivered.

"Cold, my dove? In no time you will work up quite a sweat."

"Why do you call me that?"

"What?" He asked innocently.

"Your dove?"

" 'Tis a common enough expression. Do you prefer that I cease?"

Artemis shrugged. "One of the highwaymen said the same. It makes me a little uncomfortable."

"Reminds you too much of them?" Cherry asked.

"Something like that."

Cherry bowed. "Very well, I shall no longer say it. I certainly do not wish to be compared by any means to those criminals."

Artemis nodded. He was nothing like the ruffians who had accosted her carriage. She chose the small dagger. It would make the most sense to carry. She doubted she could traipse about Town with a sword strapped to her hip. "What about this one?"

"A dagger? Good Lord, woman, why exactly do you wish to learn this?"

She noticed that his voice had deepened with genuine concern. "London is a big city. Is it not wise for a gentlewoman to learn to protect herself?"

He shifted his weight to one foot and cocked his head as he placed his hands upon his hips. "Upon my word, but any other woman, I would say no. 'Tis not wise at all. But you, Artemis Rothwell, what game do you play?" His rather shrill high voice was firmly back in place.

Artemis affected innocence. "No games, I assure you. I simply want to learn. I have never claimed a fondness for watercolors or shopping or the other things a normal gently bred miss does. I was raised with brothers and a father who encouraged me to follow in their footsteps. Fencing will actually give me a leg up on them, so to speak." And that was the truth, she thought. Just not all of it.

"What did your mother have to say?" He selected a fine sword with a slightly smaller and much less ornate handle. He handed it to her.

She reached out to take the rapier. "My mother died when I was very young. Lady Rothwell is my stepmother. My father remarried before I turned twelve. I love my stepmother dearly. Although she encouraged me in the feminine pursuits, she never discouraged me from being true to myself."

Cherry looked thoughtful. "A wise woman. Too bad my father had not her wisdom." He picked out his own sword and led her to the lush green expanse of open lawn.

"Did you not get on well with your father?" Artemis asked.

"I idolized him, but I never measured up to my brother, Charles, no matter how hard I tried."

"Oh." She imagined how difficult it must have been to live in the shadow of a favored sibling. The fact that Lord Cherrington acted rather feminine must have only contributed to the problem.

"Very well, Miss Rothwell," he said. "Let us start with a bit of stretching, and then I shall show you some basic moves. Once you have mastered the sword, we might move on to the dagger."

Artemis smiled. "Thank you, Cherry."

"You are most welcome, Artie."

After showing her several ways to stretch, Brian watched her like a hawk to ensure that she followed his lead. The fact that he enjoyed the view of her luscious form bending in abandon was not lost on him. He smiled far more than necessary for encouragement.

He started with the very basics of swordsmanship. She was a quick study, and in no time they were thrusting and parrying. She was stronger than he expected. She did not tire easily, but she did indeed sweat. Beads of perspiration trickled down her forehead.

They were due for a break. Clancy appeared with a chilled pitcher and glasses, as if mentally summoned. Brian smiled. He knew Clancy had wanted a good look at Miss Rothwell. He had told him about her request to learn to fence.

"Lemonade?" he asked.

"Please," she groaned as she sat down on a bench beside the stone table. They were shielded from the morning sunshine by an awning that jutted out from the conservatory of the townhouse. She took an offered towel from Clancy and unbuttoned the high-necked sack she wore. Brian stood transfixed as she rubbed the cloth around her neck.

Her hair, though pinned into a knot, had several strands falling down past her shoulders. The color was dark and dusky, just like her magnificent eyes that glittered from the exertion.

He realized he was staring and gave himself a mental shake. "I believe that shall do for today. It is getting late, and no doubt you will be missed if you tarry too long."

She looked down at the tiny clock brooch she wore pinned near her shoulder. "Only half past eight. I have a few moments yet. No one rouses before nine. Besides, I wish for another glass." She held out her cup, and Brian poured. Clancy had silently retreated back to the house.

"Will you tell me about Ashbourne?" He looked into her eyes. There was no discomfort there, no pining looks of lost love, and he was relieved.

"My father invited several families and eligible gentlemen for a hunting party. The Quorn is run upon Rothwell land, you know."

He cocked an eyebrow. "Impressive." He could have cared less.

"Ashbourne was one of the gentlemen. I was not in the least interested in a match or marriage with anyone, but . . ." she hesitated.

"You fell in love?"

"Heavens no." She shifted uncomfortably.

Brian sat down at a bench opposite her. "If it troubles you to speak of it, you needn't."

"No, it is not that. In fact, perhaps you might understand."

Again he raised his brow, but kept quiet, allowing her time to gather her thoughts.

"You see, because of my height and my exuberance for out-of-doors activities, I tend to feel awkward around other ladies. I am quite like a fish out of water, if you will. When Ashbourne declared his interest in me over the others, I felt compelled to compete for his attention."

Brian nodded for her to continue. Nothing shocking thus far. In fact, his heart went out to her. He remembered her shame when the Leader had ridiculed her stature that day at the holdup. It was that alone that had crumbled her confidence. That and the laughter from the others had made her limply drop her arm. The desire to find the scoundrels and bring them to justice burned anew in his breast.

"I realized that while his intent had been to pay his addresses to me, Ashbourne could not keep away from my stepmother's dearest friend, Miranda."

"Now Lady Ashbourne."

"Yes. They had a past, were once betrothed, but I did not know that at the time. Compared to Miranda, I am nothing, but I wanted to be something and so I accepted Ashbourne for all the wrong reasons. When I found out that he truly loved Miranda and she him, the rest you have no doubt heard from the Waterton-Smythe sisters."

Brian took hold of her hand. "Artemis, you are indeed something very special. Do not ever think you are not."

She pulled her hand away. "Come now, Cherry. I am no beauty."

"You underestimate your charm, my—uh, dear."

"Ah, but I also know my worth. The Rothwell dowry is sizable." She stood, her cup empty, ready to leave.

"So I have heard." He chuckled. There was no arguing with the girl. She thought herself plain even though she was anything but plain. Her features were not delicate enough for her to ever be considered pretty, but her appeal was undeniable. She needed only confidence.

Fencing had a tendency to give that. He was glad he was teaching her. He hoped to teach her other things in time. "Our time is at an end. Shall we meet again tomorrow morning?"

"Yes." She moved toward her townhouse, but then she turned. "Thank you, Cherry," she said with genuine appreciation. Then she darted through the waist-high wall of boxwood that separated his lawns from that of Lady Ashbourne's.

"A charming girl." Clancy appeared to gather the swords to take them inside.

Brian continued to stare in the direction Artemis had gone. "Indeed."

"A bit unconventional," Clancy offered.

"Completely."

"Why does she wish to learn swordplay?"

"I'm not entirely certain, but Miss Rothwell has a score to settle with the highwaymen. I fear she just might be making plans inside that handsome head of hers that could land her in a heap of trouble."

"Perhaps you should enlist her aid in your search for the men's identities but make it appear that you are helping her," Clancy said.

Brian turned then. "Are you insane? What if she found out about me?"

"My lord, what information have you gained thus far?"

Brian mulled over the question. He had found out very little indeed. His silence was answer enough.

"How better to keep your alter ego a secret from her than to offer your assistance."

"Clancy, I shall give the matter some thought," Brian said. "But for now, I must wash and change. I am headed for Lord Sidmouth's office and then onto a breakfast held at the Collington estate in Kensington."

"Very well, my lord."

Artemis made it back into her room minutes before her stepmother knocked upon her door. She stuffed the plain dress she had just taken off under the pillows of her bed. Wrapping a robe over her chemise, she called out, "Come in."

"Artemis dear, your father wishes to return home so we shall be leaving shortly."

"Oh?" Artemis gestured for her stepmother to come closer. "Mama," she whispered. "Perhaps now that you two are headed home, I should report the theft of your ring to the Runners."

Her stepmother nodded. "Your father noticed that I have not worn it. I cannot wear mittens to bed, you know. And I told him a dreadful fib. I said that I might have left it at Rothwell Park. Artemis, you must, indeed, report it. Perhaps, Miranda will go with you."

"Has she told Ashbourne?"

"I do not think so. But she may once we are safe at home, if she must. I do hope the ring turns up. Here." Her stepmother gave Artemis several pound notes. "If a pawnbroker does happen upon it, try to buy it back. If this is not enough, then use it as a deposit for him to hold it, until we return to fetch you at the end of the Season."

Artemis folded the notes neatly before placing them in a locked compartment in her desk. "How soon do you leave?"

"After we break our fast. Miranda has ordered a large spread in the morning room."

"I will join you as soon as I am dressed," Artemis said.

"Perfect." Her stepmother reached out her hand to touch Artemis' forehead. "Are you feeling ill, dear? Your color is high and your skin feels clammy."

"Too many covers while I slept, Mama. I became overheated."

Her stepmother pulled her into an embrace. "I will miss you so. Just think, you might find yourself a gentleman to marry and then you will truly be on your own."

Artemis squeezed her tight. She was not opposed to the idea of marriage; only she had not a clue as to who might present himself as an acceptable candidate. A merry pair of blue eyes belonging to Lord Cherrington danced in her thoughts. She shut her eyes tight against such folly. Her father would never, ever approve of the man!

*   *   *

"Come, we must hurry," Miranda said. "We do not wish to be late to the Collingtons."

Artemis followed Miranda into the office belonging to the Bow Street Runners. They descended a few steps that emptied into a vast foyer. At the opposite wall, a wrought iron gate surrounded a square space that appeared to make up a trial area. Doors leading to offices were closed, their secrets kept from public viewing.

Clerks scurried about and she stood quietly next to Miranda as she used her position in society to gain an audience with Mr. John Stafford, the chief clerk. He was in charge of the Runners and reported directly to the secretary of the Home Office.

Artemis gave her testimony regarding the events that took place involving the theft of the Rothwell ring. She described the ring in detail and also stated her stepmother's desire to keep the knowledge of the robbery from her father, Lord Rothwell, for the time being.

They were treated with respect and given every assurance that the Runners were doing all that was possible to catch the thieves. But in the end, they were escorted out the door quickly as if they were a nuisance. Artemis fairly seethed with frustration.

"Do not worry, dear." Miranda patted her hand. "Things will be put to rights, you shall see."

"Yes, but will Mama have her ring back?"

Miranda had no answer, or perhaps she was saved the need to answer by Lord Cherrington nearly bumping into them in the lobby.

"Lord Cherrington," Miranda said. "What a pleasant surprise."

"Indeed."

Artemis noticed that he looked flushed through the cheeks and his ears were red. "What brings you to the Runners' office?"

Cherry looked thoughtful a moment.

"Truly, it is none of our concern," Miranda said to cover the awkward moment.

"I do not mind, Lady Ashbourne. The truth is that I am continually looking for any information regarding my brother's death. The bandits remain at large, more's the pity."

Artemis felt the heat of shame wash over her. She had forgotten that Cherry might seek justice for his brother's death just as they sought it for their theft. She had been so wrapped up with her own loss, that she had been shortsighted with her friend. After today's lesson in swords, she felt confident in considering Lord Cherrington a friend.

She reached out and touched his forearm. "I am so sorry, Cherry. These highwaymen are dastardly indeed, and yet Bow Street has nothing to offer by way of catching them." She let her ire have its due. "They act as if they do not care that my family's betrothal ring, in the Rothwell family for nearly a hundred years, is gone!"

"Now, Artemis," Miranda said soothingly. "They are doing all they can what with the other crimes committed in this vast city."

"It is not enough, not for me and certainly not for Lord Cherrington." She cast a look of sympathy his way. "I feel so helpless, surely there is something we can do?"

"We *are* doing everything," Miranda said. "Perhaps we might make another round of the pawnbroker shops on the morrow."

Artemis sighed. "Yes, of course."

"I would be delighted to escort you, Miss Rothwell, with Lady Ashbourne's permission."

"Would you?" Artemis asked. "I would truly appreciate it."

"Indeed," Miranda said. "We all would."

"Very well, I shall collect you in the morning, say eleven o'clock?"

Artemis smiled. "Let's make it ten."

"Very well," he bowed.

"Come, Artemis." Miranda took her arm. "Lord Cherrington, do forgive our hurried departure, but we are expected at the Collingtons' for breakfast."

"'Pon rep, so am I. I shall bid you good day then until we meet again at the Collingtons'." Cherry made an exquisite bow.

Artemis and Miranda made their exit, but she looked back as Cherry spoke to one of the officers. She felt heaviness in her heart considering that she had welcomed a kiss from one of the highwaymen when they were capable of hurting another.

Artemis decided there and then that she would indeed find a way to retrieve the Rothwell ring. If the Leader of the highwaymen still had it, the only way she could get it back was to deal directly with him. The question was how?

The Collington Estate on the outskirts of Kensington was beautiful indeed. The day proved fine with mild temperatures and blue skies dotted by puffy white clouds that hid the sun for only moments at a time. The manor was not overly large but built with lovely stone the color of ivory. The parkland surrounding the main house was vast indeed, complete with a pond that had access directly to the Thames.

Artemis felt her nerves tighten as the carriage pulled into line on the main drive. She had dressed carefully, wanting to look right. She hoped to blend in perfectly rather than stand out. After Cherry had mentioned that she could improve on her mode of dress, she wondered what he would think of the gown she chose. She fiddled with the white flounce of her cotton voile morning dress.

"You look lovely," Miranda whispered as if sensing her unease.

"Indeed you do," Lord Ashbourne added. "I shall have two striking women on my arm when I walk into this party."

Artemis smiled. Miranda beamed. The two of them appeared quite comfortable with each other, even if Ashbourne tended to hover about his wife at society functions. He was a bit protective, Miranda had once told her. But she did not seem to mind overmuch. Once the Season was at an end, the two planned to remove to Ash Manor for the rest of the year.

Artemis had overheard her father making plans with Ashbourne for several hunts throughout the late summer and autumn. No doubt, she would see them often. She experienced a pang of regret that Cherry did not enjoy the hunt. She would simply have to write to him after the Season was over. Unless she married and set up a home of her own, as her stepmother said. Her husband would hardly condone letters written to another man.

She considered the gentlemen who had called upon her at Miranda's townhouse. So far the only gentleman she knew her father would approve of was Lord Cole. But he did not quite realize that Artemis was female. She liked being considered almost an equal and even enjoyed their lively conversations of horses, Tattersalls, and hunting, but she was beginning to see that there was more in life than that.

Lord Ranton and Mr. Mellowby saw only the Rothwell dowry instead of the lady that came with it. Neither one held any interest for her. It was too early in the Season to make any permanent judgments. It was still quite probable that she might remain completely unattached just as Harriet had done.

Once outside on the lawns, Artemis tried to relax. She would not make a fool of herself as she had done at the Waterton-Smythe ball. She would act with complete decorum. Several couples played lawn chess a few yards from the food tents. Others rowed about in small boats on the pond. What caught Artemis' eye was an area set up for archery. She breathed a bit easier. She could at least enjoy one area of amusement at the Collington breakfast.

"Come, Artemis, and meet the hostess," Miranda said. Her arm remained firmly linked in Ashbourne's.

Artemis followed, feeling much like a third wheel. She made her bows to their hostess, nibbled on a tart, and drank tea until finally Harriet appeared.

"Artemis," Harriet said. "Let us make up a team against someone. Several people are gathering at the archery targets."

Artemis glanced at Miranda, who nodded with

agreement that she might be excused. Once out from under the tea tent, Artemis turned to Harriet. "I was wondering when you would arrive."

"We have only just pulled in. I could hardly wait to find you. With your prowess at bow and arrows, we are sure to catch the gentlemen's notice."

"Why, Harriet, is there someone you wish to attract?"

"Of course, silly. Why else would I put myself through yet another Season?"

Artemis had not really given it much thought. She believed that Harriet Whitlow was content with her single state. She was a pretty young lady with a considerable marriage portion and good lineage. Her father was an earl. Artemis had never considered that her friend had trouble attracting gentlemen. Her dance cards thus far had always been filled. She was highly regarded by all. "Is there a gentleman in particular that you wish to pursue?"

Harriet looked guilty and blushed.

"Who is it? Someone I know?"

"Of course." Harriet would not look at her.

Artemis stopped walking. "Who?"

Harriet stopped as well. "Promise you will not tell him."

"Why would I do that?"

"With the intention of helping me, of course."

"Very well, I promise."

Harriet looked about to make certain there was no one within earshot. Her face turned red and she coughed. "Promise you will not laugh."

"Why would I laugh?" Artemis suddenly wondered if Harriet cared for Lord Cherrington.

"Because." Harriet stepped closer and whispered. "It is Mr. Clasby."

Artemis was amazed to feel real relief that Harriet had not mentioned Cherry, but it was short-lived. Relief gave way to pity, since Mr. Clasby was a rake. The whispered gossip was that he currently carried on a rather torrid affair with a married lady. She felt horrible for her friend, who was bound to be disappointed or worse. "He is a bit of rogue, you know."

Harriet lifted her chin. "I know. Perhaps he might change his ways with the right woman by his side."

Artemis sighed. She could not possibly believe that woman was her friend, but she kept her thoughts to herself. Mr. Clasby was a friend, but considering his character, he would not make the best husband and certainly not one for a sweet young lady like Harriet Whitlow.

"Come, Artie." Harriet pulled her hand. "They are forming teams."

Chapter Six

*H*e seethed with envy and frustration as he watched her. The Rothwell giantess moved smoothly within society's circles when she had no business being accepted by the *ton*. Her social indiscretions mounted, and yet all were dismissed as if she was somehow above the proper codes of behavior set forth by the same haute monde that had condemned his father and kept him slightly on the fringes. He was tolerated while the Rothwell chit was welcomed with open arms.

Overhearing Lady Jersey's approval of Artemis Rothwell after the girl had waltzed without permission with that ridiculous excuse for a man, Lord Cherrington, had made him purple with wrath. The utter unfairness of it irked him as nothing else had. And now the girl displayed her ability with bow and arrow as if it were commonplace to beat gentlemen at their own sport. It was unnatural in the extreme, and yet no one seemed to care.

But *he* cared.

Soon enough he would get even. He knew she

searched for the ring that he took. He had heard it from one of the pawnbrokers he frequented. For that reason alone, he held onto it. He'd keep it just to spite her. Somehow he'd expose Artemis Rothwell as the despicable hoyden he knew her to be.

Artemis pulled back the bowstring and let her arrow fly. It hit very near the center of the target. The corners of her mouth involuntarily lifted. She was making mice feet of Mr. Mellowby's attempts to beat her. Harriet had since gone off with Mr. Clasby after they had been beaten as a team. Artemis had planned to go with them, but Lord Ranton had challenged her to an individual match.

She could hardly refuse after he had good-naturedly taunted her. He had witnessed her prowess, and said such a performance could hardly be repeated. Lord Ranton had teased that she could not best him at bow and arrow—her earlier win had simply been a lark.

No sooner did she beat Lord Ranton and send him away to laughingly swallow his words, than Lord Cole approached to give it a go. And now Mr. Mellowby tried to match her, but to no avail. She was clearly in the lead. A small group of gentlemen had gathered, and she overheard a wager or two being placed. She concentrated on her aim for her last shot, hoping for a dead-center bull's-eye.

"Look, Lord Cherrington, 'tis Miss Rothwell making a cake of herself." The feminine voice was loud enough for all to hear.

Artemis overheard the cruel comment just before she let go of the bow, and her arrow missed its mark by landing in the second ring. She still trounced Mr. Mellowby, much to the man's red-faced shame, but she had so wanted to end with a bull's-eye.

She turned to spy Cherry with five ladies surrounding him. Two of them were the Waterton-Smythe sisters. She rolled her eyes.

"Nonsense, *ma chérie*," Cherrington cajoled one of the sisters. "She is simply showing her skill. And you are showing your claws because she has stolen the attentions of many gentlemen."

Instead of taking pride in Cherry's words, she felt like a fool. She had done it again. She had let her inane desire to win spoil the image she was trying to portray to the *ton*. She was a lady, but instead of acting as one, she must look terribly like a romp.

Several of the gentlemen laughed when they overheard Cherrington's scold. And then Lord Cole piped up, "Have a go, Cherrington. See if you can not usurp our Queen of Arrows."

Brian flashed a quick glance at Artemis. He felt the pain that she tried so hard to hide. She looked uncomfortable and awkward, yet she could not turn tail and run or the Waterton-Smythe harpy would have won.

Brian thought quickly. If he could actually beat her, then perhaps he might save Artemis' name from being bandied about as the Queen of Arrows from club to club. He had the distinct feeling that Artemis had not anticipated such notoriety, nor did she look as though she welcomed it.

He disengaged himself from one young lady hanging upon his arm and bowed. "Pon rep, I shall try." He gingerly took a pinch of stuff from his jewel-encrusted box and sneezed. Wiping his nose delicately with a lace handkerchief earned him several guffaws.

"Any time now, Cherrington," Lord Cole teased.

"Of course." Brian made a show of sneezing once more, giving Artemis ample time to regain her composure.

"I hope you are good," she whispered under her breath when finally he retrieved a quiver of arrows from her.

"Indeed, I am not bang-up prime, but I shall endeavor to do my best. I expect no less from you." He gave her an encouraging nod. He hoped she would not be obvious if she threw off her game. A larger audience had gathered, and Brian knew that Artemis was nervous. Well, she had landed into this kettle of fish all by herself—he'd see what he could do to get her out.

Artemis won the draw to go first. She made steady her shaking elbow as she drew back on the bowstring, then she let her arrow fly with a resounding thud. She must lose, yet she must not appear to be trying to lose. Cherry had made that much clear. Again, she owed him gratitude for saving her from more disgrace, if he could pull off besting her.

Her arrow landed squarely in the middle ring, though not dead center. "Your turn, Lord Cherrington," she said a little breathlessly.

"Egad, but you are good," he said with genuine appreciation. It made her smile, despite their circumstances.

She watched closely as he took his stance, looking ridiculous with his shirt points so high it was nearly impossible for him to turn his head. Artemis wondered how he managed to see over them. She stifled the urge to chew her nails and instead, clasped her hands firmly behind her back.

He pulled back his elbow and took aim. Artemis noticed that his form was not at all bad. Indeed he looked rather sure of himself. He let go and his arrow sailed through the air to land just below her own. He had hit the third ring.

They played for half of an hour. Artemis had effectively thrown off her aim just enough to allow Cherry to take the lead. His aim, however, was splendid, so by all appearances he looked as if he was beating her soundly. The last set of arrows remained, and Lord Cherrington led by four points.

The heat of competition washed over Artemis, making her pulse race. She could only hope to tie with a bull's-eye. Surely a tie would exonerate her for defeating three gentlemen, she thought carelessly. She could not keep her desire to win effectively at bay. There must indeed be something wrong with her to loathe losing so badly, even when it was important for her to do so.

It was her turn. She glanced at Cherry, who gave her an insolent wink. It served only to goad her further into aiming for the tie. She stood with her back straight and her face turned toward the target. She pulled her arrow with every ounce of concentration she possibly had.

A hush settled over the crowd that stood by watching. Sweat beaded along her brow as she focused with all her might on hitting the bull's-eye. She let her arrow fly. It hit the very edge of the black dot.

It was not dead center, but it earned her the required points to tie with Cherry.

His aim needed to be as good or better in order to beat her. She gave him a cheeky grin, but his brow furrowed with concern. He did not appear happy with her choice of action. Cherry squinted at the target, then without preamble, he divested himself of his deep mulberry coat to reveal a silver waistcoat striped with gold.

"Come on, Cherrington, win this for the men," Lord Cole cheered.

"Here, here." Many of the men standing about agreed until the ladies present joined in with their own good wishes.

Artemis caught sight of Harriet standing beside Mr. Clasby, and both wore tight expressions. She turned her attention back to Cherry. He was as slender as he was tall. She noted that his posture was good when he did not mince. He straightened his rather broad shoulders before pulling the bowstring. Artemis found herself admiring the way the wiry muscles of his thighs and calves tensed under the second skin of his Wellington pantaloons. She was so distracted by this, that she missed his shot. She looked up once she heard the gasps of the crowd.

Lord Cherrington did not hit the center of the bull's eye. He had done better than that. He had effectively split her arrow, something she had rarely seen done. She felt herself smiling broadly, and then she burst into laughter.

"Oh, well done," she finally said.

But Cherry did not hear her. Surrounded by several ladies, he was nearly knocked over when they tried to take his arm. Artemis quickly turned her attention toward the gentlemen, but they busied themselves with finalizing the wagers.

Harriet was at her arm. "Lucky for you, Lord Cherrington won."

Artemis felt oddly deflated. "I suppose you have the right of it."

"Of course I do. You cannot be known to beat some of the finest Corinthians at bow and arrow and expect to hold your head up in society. Artie, I thought you knew better."

Artemis hung her head. "I do."

Harriet looped her arm through her friend's. "Cheer up. Mr. Clasby assured me that most of the guests did not actually watch the archery competition, although it is sure to be remarked upon. There have been other distractions present today. An overturned rowboat with the rescue of a lady who not only could not swim, but failed to wear a chemise under her dress captured much of the attention away from you."

"Where are Miranda and Ashbourne?" Artemis asked. She had promised to make her parents proud by making it easy on Miranda to bring her out.

"She is helping the young lady change along with Lady Collington. Ashbourne has not left his wife's side, although he now waits in the hall. I think Lord Collington was casting flirtatious looks Miranda's way, and Lord Ashbourne was bound to protect his wife from any unwanted advances."

"Oh, dear," Artemis said. "Poor Ashbourne."

"Poor Miranda," Harriet said and then laughed.

Artemis joined her. Perhaps she had not made a

mull of everything after all. Even so, she was relieved that Cherry had convincingly won.

"Miranda, please forgive me for my actions today," Artemis said as they rode in Ashbourne's carriage on their way to Lady Jersey's home in Berkeley Square.

"Honestly, Artemis, I do not think you fared poorly at all," Miranda explained. "Firstly, you did nothing horribly wrong. The archery lanes had been set up for enjoyment. True, you would have been wiser to have not beaten three sporting gentlemen in a row, but Lord Cherrington put that to rights."

"You let him win, did you not?" Ashbourne asked with a smile.

"Indeed, I did. But his aim was quite true on his own merit."

"Besides," Miranda went on, ignoring her husband's interruption. "Poor Lucinda Bronwell's display coming out of the pond firmly cast your slight indiscretion in the shade. She looked quite naked."

Ashbourne grinned. "Quite."

Miranda proceeded to playfully swat her husband, and Artemis laughed with ease. She had not disgraced her hosts. There had been little time to discuss the matter after they returned from the Collingtons' as they had been invited to the Jerseys' for an exclusive dinner party. Artemis had stewed over her actions needlessly.

"Lady Jersey is fond of you, Artemis," Miranda added. "She expressly asked that you come tonight as well. I think you remind her a little of herself. You both have your height in common."

"We are both plain," Artemis chimed in, trying to sound light, but her voice cracked. She could not erase the image of five beauties hanging upon Cherry's every word.

"You are not plain," Miranda admonished. "You are a handsome young woman, Artemis. Carry yourself with pride. Take a lesson from our own Lady Jersey in deportment."

"Indeed," Ashbourne added. "The Incomparables come and go, and who's to remember them once they are wed and beyond a gentleman's touch. A woman of fine character and strength is remembered always."

"Evan, that was lovely," Miranda said.

"Such is the truth for you as well, my dear."

Artemis' face grew warm, and the carriage suddenly seemed too small for the three of them. Ashbourne and Miranda were still newly wed after all. They never missed a moment to make sheep's eyes at one another.

Fortunately, they pulled into the line of carriages, and Artemis peered out the window to see whom she might recognize. Harriet and her family had been invited, so Artemis knew she would have at least one friend in attendance. Lord Cherrington might also show, considering his family's friendship with Lady Jersey.

When their carriage door was opened by one of Lady Jersey's footmen, Artemis got out first. They walked up the steps into the grand hall, where a distinguished-looking butler took their pelisses and Ashbourne's top hat and gloves. They entered the drawing room, and Artemis was awed at the number in attendance for what was described as an *intimate* dinner with friends. But then, a leader of society must have many friends, she thought.

"Miss Rothwell, welcome. And how wonderful you look." Their hostess's smile was genuine and full of warmth. Perhaps what Ashbourne said might indeed be true.

"Thank you, Lady Jersey." Artemis curtsied properly without even the slightest wobble. She felt honored that Lady Jersey had singled her out. "Might I say the same of you?"

Lady Jersey laughed then added, "Of course you may, dear, but what I find exhilarating is that I have heard you trounced Lord Cole at arrows this afternoon. Now, that, Miss Rothwell, is a feat on which to be congratulated."

Artemis felt herself blush to her toes, but she was also immensely relieved. If Lady Jersey was not offended, then who could possibly hold this afternoon's antics against her? "I am humbled and grateful for your kind words, ma'am."

"Oh, you are a delight." Lady Jersey turned to introduce her to the earl. "Jersey, dear. This is Miss Artemis Rothwell, Beldon's daughter." Then to Artemis, she added. "Jersey has been breeding horses for years, but he keeps his eye on Rothwell stock."

"Really?" Artemis' chest swelled as she spoke to the fifth Earl of Jersey about horses and her father's successes with Castlestone's sire. Lady Jersey turned to Miranda and Ashbourne. When the three of them finally moved on, Artemis held her head a bit higher than when she had first walked in.

"Miss Rothwell." Cherry bowed before her, then

looked her up and down with his quizzing glass. "What has you looking like the cat that got the cream?"

"Cherry." Artemis looped her arm through his as easily as she would any friend. "Lady Jersey actually congratulated me on beating Lord Cole at arrows! Can you imagine? I am not a disgrace."

"Dearest kitten," he said with a pat on her arm. "You worried about this all afternoon, did you not?"

Artemis did not confess to her dismals. "I must thank you again for putting in a good word for me with Lady Jersey. Somehow, I'd wager that it was you who told her about the archery competition." She noticed that his face powder had been applied with a heavier hand this evening. He had made a false mole at the corner of his mouth, calling attention to his well-formed lips.

Cherry bowed with a flourish of his slender hand. "Your appreciation is graciously accepted."

When he stood, Artemis took in what he was wearing. He was garbed in a black velvet coat that covered a shimmering waistcoat that looked silver, and then depending on how the light shined upon him, it turned blue. His knee-length breeches were also of black velvet under which silvery stockings covered muscular calves leading to feet that settled into black velvet pumps.

"Are you quite finished with your inspection?" he asked with a wicked grin.

"My goodness, you are very shiny this evening," Artemis breathed.

"I shall endeavor to take that as a compliment.

While you look ravishing. Much better than the white gown you wore this morning."

"What was wrong with what I wore this morning?" She ignored his compliment, since it was more important to understand why the dress she wore earlier had been unacceptable.

"Perfectly suitable, but terribly dull. Ruffles don't suit you."

"There were only two," Artemis protested.

"Even so." He winked at her. "Flowing drapes with no flounces or beribboned gatherings to get in the way of your magnificent height look much better on you."

Artemis felt her spine stiffen. "I am a tall Meg, am I not?"

"And every inch of you perfect." He smiled sweetly. "Now come, let us make the rounds."

Artemis let herself be pulled about the room by Lord Cherrington, who introduced her to several gentlemen and ladies. For someone new to the *ton*, he was acquainted with many. She noted that she felt completely at ease upon his arm. Perhaps it was because he was a few inches taller than she, or perhaps it was because he did not try to ignore her stature as many did. Instead, he openly remarked upon it, praised it in fact.

"Artemis, how lovely that color is on you," Harriet whispered as she came upon them. "It can only be described as buttery."

"Rich and delicious," Cherry added with a wink, then said, "ah, ladies, forgive my premature departure, but I am being hailed." He bowed. "Your servant."

"An interesting man," Harriet said as she watched him walk away.

Artemis merely shook her head. The woman that hailed him was as beautiful as she was petite. Artemis looked away. "He is that."

"I do not see Mr. Clasby here tonight," Harriet said.

"Nor is Mr. Mellowby or Lord Ranton." Artemis did not wish to be the one to break it to her friend, who should have known that Mr. Clasby, though socially acceptable, was not exactly welcome in the highest echelons of gentle company. His reputation with married ladies precluded him from some functions.

"Honestly, you should not pay either gentleman much heed," Harriet said.

Nor should you, Artemis thought, but instead said, "I do not exactly have a pool of men vying to be my dance partners. Those two gentlemen along with Lord Cole, Cherrington, and Mr. Clasby are the only fellows who will dance with me."

"Perhaps that will soon change," Harriet said, then she lowered her voice to a whisper. "My papa stopped at his club tonight, and you were quite the topic of conversation."

Artemis' heart dropped to her feet. "Oh, dear."

"You are being hailed as quite the good sport and a great gun to boot." Harriet smiled.

Artemis realized that the two of them were nearly alone in their corner of the drawing room. "Harriet, I have a favor to ask."

"Of course, dear, anything."

"But you must promise not to breathe a word of it, whether or not you agree."

Harriet drew closer and whispered. "Of course, whatever is it?"

"I need to stage a carriage accident so that I might meet up with the highwaymen again. Perhaps you might procure a carriage for us to use?" She watched her friend's color fade.

"You want to do what?" Now Harriet's cheeks turned a splotchy pink.

"Come now, Harriet. Many of the other ladies are doing it."

"Goodness, Artie. Surely you have enough male attention."

Artemis sighed. "That is not the reason for my request."

"Then why?" But realization immediately dawned on Harriet's face. "The Rothwell ring."

"Exactly. I have to get it back. I am convinced the only way is to meet the bandits again and offer to purchase the ring back from him."

"When did you think up this plan?"

"It has been rolling about for a time now, but only just became clear when I overheard some of the other ladies talking of doing the very same thing this afternoon."

"I do not know. Let me think on it."

"Do not take too long. I need your help." Artemis squeezed Harriet's hand just before Lord Cole approached them.

"Ladies," Lord Cole said. "What mischief do you plan with your heads so close together?"

Artemis laughed to cover Harriet's definite look of guilt. "Why, how to best you at another sport, of course," she said as she took Lord Cole's arm.

"My dear, Miss Rothwell, I begin to think you could rival a gentleman at nearly anything." Lord Cole offered his other arm to Harriet.

"Lord Cole, I take that as the highest compliment," Artemis lied.

Brian sat amid his court of eligible young ladies while they awaited the announcement of dinner. There were nearly eight of them vying for his advice on the latest fashions and which bonnets looked best atop which hairstyles. It was a small price to pay for information.

Since the start of his Season, as it were, Brian had been discreetly asking these ladies about their various choices for suitors, as well as where, when, and if these gentlemen had called upon them. It did not take long to earn their trust or loosen their tongues, as he had become a confidant.

Still, there were a few who were not opposed to snagging him for their matrimonial prize. Two of them were the Waterton-Smythe sisters, to his utmost distaste. But he could not alienate a single female, for fear that they might unwittingly hold the key to the highwaymen's identities.

And so he teased and cajoled each lady until he heard some tidbit of information he thought might be important. And when he found a quiet moment in which he could excuse himself, Brian made sure he jotted down every *on-dit* he had gleaned into a tiny notebook he kept safely tucked into his waistcoat pocket.

So far, he was more confused than ever.

Chapter Seven

Artemis crept through the boxwood hedge that separated the yards belonging to Miranda's townhouse with those of Cherry's. She spotted him testing two swords, shifting them from one hand to the other. As expected he was dressed in buff pantaloons and a white lawn shirt. The morning air was heavy with moisture. Artemis assumed the heat was the reason Cherry chose not to wear a fastidiously tied cravat to support a terribly high collar.

"I think it might rain," she said to let him know she was there.

Cherry turned around and smiled. "Indeed, it just might."

Artemis shook her head. He still wore face powder! She thought he would look much better without it, but she did not have the nerve to tell him so. What if he hid some terrible birthmark underneath all that rice powder? "What shall I learn today?" she asked.

"Since we have already gone over the basic stances, perhaps we might actually duel a bit?"

Artemis grinned when he produced the two light

dueling swords he had been testing. "Have you ever been in an actual duel?"

"Never," he said. With a wink he added, "Who would ever wish to meet me at dawn?" He handed her the sword by the tip of the blade as it bent toward her, its guarded handle ready for her to grasp.

"Let me think of possible circumstances. Have you never tangled with a lady intended for another?"

Cherry feigned mock horror. "Heaven's no. Miss Rothwell, surely you know me better than that. Let us go over the moves we learned the other morning."

"Hmmmm." She thought harder as they slowly practiced their lunges, parries, and ripostes. "Cherry, have you never done anything wrong?"

He thought a moment before answering. "Other than not joining the military as my father wished, no, not really. Compared to the life my brother led, I am quite dull." He lunged toward her.

"No one could accuse you of being dull." She moved to parry in prime.

"Perhaps, but even so, I could not find favor in my father's eyes. At the same time, no matter what Charles did, what scrape he fell into or act of dishonor he perpetrated, he could not dim the shining approval he had from my father." He reacted in riposte.

"I see." Artemis counter-riposted as he had shown her. "I am fortunate that I am confident in my father's love, although I cannot help but think that I am at times a disappointment as a lady. Perhaps I am too manly."

"Never." He thrust forward. "But then, I fear I might be too feminine."

Artemis could not help but giggle. "Who would ever say that?"

Cherry laughed out loud until they both dissolved into a fit of amusement that kept them from practicing. "Come," he said. "I will show you a couple more defensive moves, and then we shall have a go at it. I think you are ready. There are protective tips on the blades. Neither of us should get hurt."

Artemis licked her lips before nodding. Her blood pumped with excitement. She watched Cherrington's every move as he demonstrated more stances and thrusts. Finally they engaged in actual swordplay, and regardless of how hard she concentrated, she could not keep the smile from her face. She loved every minute.

They moved swiftly, thrusting and counterthrusting in attack. She knew only the first few movements to parry, but used them well as he counterparried. After a solid twenty minutes, they were both overheated and in need of water.

"Shall we?" He gestured for her to go before him to the table under the awning that had been laid out with towels and refreshments. "You are quite good," he said. "Is there nothing you cannot do?" He poured a glass of water and offered it to her.

She drank thirstily then answered, "I cannot watercolor and I cannot sing. I play the pianoforte with a small measure of competence, but I am by no means accomplished."

He burst out laughing again, and Artemis loved

the sound. For a dandy, he had a wonderfully masculine laugh.

She finished her water and stood. "Can you teach me more moves?"

It was an innocent enough question, but Brian felt his insides turn to fire as he considered just what he'd like to teach her. She wore a simple cotton morning gown that was damp with sweat, making the bodice cling to her full bosom rather nicely. Her hair had been simply done into a thick braid, and it hung down her back. She looked fresh with her cheeks pink from exertion. Standing there staring at her like an idiot, he was bowled over by how badly he wanted her.

"Cherry?" Her brow furrowed.

"Yes, of course. Let us return to the swords." He set down his glass. They set off for the area of play, where he did indeed show her more offensive and defensive movements. He held back and let her take the offensive. He was impressed at how quickly she caught on and how long she endured. She was not a pampered miss used to lazing about. She was strong and sure. When the first few drops of rain fell, they both ignored it, but the deluge that followed completely interrupted their exercise.

"Come." Without a moment's thought, Brian grabbed her hand and pulled her under the awning. As they both laughed from the drenching, it felt only natural to pull her into his arms.

Artemis returned Cherry's friendly embrace as her laughter faded. She had almost touched him with the tip of her sword before the downpour. With a lighthearted taunt ready to deliver from her lips, she looked up into his darkened blue eyes and became serious in an instant.

He pulled her a little closer, and Artemis automatically stiffened her spine. Dear Lord, she thought, surely he was not going to kiss her!

"Cherry," she said with a warning tone.

"Brian." His voice was a mere whisper.

"What?" She placed her hands upon his shoulders, ready to push him away, but she was distracted by the mass of whipcord lean muscle she felt there. It did not help her resolve when she noticed the dark spattering of hair and the defined sinew of his chest, since his shirt had become transparent from the rain.

"My name is Brian." He spoke without his usual lilting drawl or shrill voice, and the sound was indeed intoxicating. His mouth brushed lightly against her own, as if he tested her reaction.

Her body, flooded with odd sensations when he drew her against him, did not listen when her brain frantically warned her to move away. Her head grew light as his lips settled more firmly onto her mouth. She tried to back up, but he had her pinned against the pole of the awning. Her eyes closed. Lightning struck somewhere, and she swore the very ground moved.

Brian was just about to deepen this insanely agreeable kiss when he heard her gasp for air. He felt her start to panic and pulled back. The wild look in her eyes took him by surprise. She was scared to death. Artemis Rothwell, who rode like an Amazon warrior and shot arrows better than he imagined even the goddess Diana could, was just about frightened to pieces.

He stepped back from her to give her some space as she gulped a deep breath. "Artie," he said. His hand rubbed her shoulder. "Are you all right?"

"I have to go." And then she was gone, running like a wild hare across his lawns, through the boxwood and into Lady Ashbourne's townhouse.

Artemis stripped off her wet gown with shaking hands and wrapped herself in a robe before pulling the bell to order a hot bath. What on earth had just happened! One minute they had been laughing and having a grand time and the next he was kissing her with indecent abandon, making her turn hot and cold at the same time.

Artemis paced the floor of her chamber. It was not to be borne. Lord Cherrington, Brian was his Christian name, was a fop! He was a terribly feminine man who knew more about ladies' fashion then she did. And he did not even hunt! Her father would have an apoplexy.

The memory of Cherrington's hard body pressed so close to hers washed over her with a renewed flush of heat. She pressed both her hands to her warm face. She had been kissed all of three times in her life: once on a dare from a local boy when she was thirteen, once by Ashbourne in front of her parents, and then once by that pesky, tall Highwayman. None of them had the sheer impact of Cherry's buss. What was she going to do?

She took deep calming breaths. There was nothing to do. She stopped pacing. Cherry had not declared himself of any intentions. He simply gave into a temptation, since they had been so familiar with each other. That was all it was.

She hoped.

Her maid popped into her room, and Artemis bid her to fetch hot water for a bath. She quickly explained that she had been in the courtyard and had got caught in the rain. She needed a good soak to figure out how to act when she saw Cherry again. Brian, she mused. He had a nice name, but Cherry suited him better.

Brian was shown to the drawing room of Lady Ashbourne's townhouse by the competent if unfriendly butler. "Good day, Lady Ashbourne." Brian bowed once he was announced.

"Lord Cherrington, do come in and sit down. You must be here to take Artemis to the pawnshop." She nodded for the butler to send for Miss Rothwell.

"Indeed I am." Brian sat down with a flourish. "And how is Lord Ashbourne?"

"Very well, I thank you. He is at Parliament this morning."

"Ah yes. Please give my thanks to your husband again for introducing me to the hallowed halls of the House of Lords. I believe I will wait and take my place there next year when I can better concentrate."

Lady Ashbourne smiled.

Brian sat back in an attempt to patiently wait for Artemis. "I thought we might make the rounds of several pawnshops if that is convenient."

"That would be wonderful. The dear girl would go every day, if she could, she is that desperate to get it back. A terrible experience, that holdup. I think Artemis was a little shaken by it. Thank you for helping us with this. It is greatly appreciated."

Brian bowed his head. "Indeed, she must have been." He remembered too well what she had been through and how bravely she had acted. But then, everything had happened fast. She must have been in a state of shock to have not reacted to his first simple kiss.

Nothing like today.

He did not know if that bode well for him or ill. He did not think ladies were supposed to be so afraid of a kiss, but then Artemis was no ordinary lady.

The silence stretched on, and Brian tapped his fingertips upon his knee.

"I honestly do not know what is keeping her," Lady Ashbourne explained.

"No matter." Brian stopped drumming his fingers, but soon his leg twitched. He hoped Artemis did not fear facing him.

"Lord Cherrington," Artemis said breathlessly as she entered the drawing room. "I beg your pardon for keeping you waiting."

"Not at all." Brian let his gaze linger over her a moment longer than necessary, then he gave her a friendly wink to put her at ease. "I am here to take you to the pawnbroker shops as promised."

"Indeed." Artemis looked anywhere but at him.

Lady Ashbourne appeared to have noticed the awkward silence. "Good luck," she said with brazen double meaning.

Brian held out his arm for Artemis to take. "Shall we?"

She took it after a slight hesitation, and then turned her head to Lady Ashbourne. "I doubt we will be gone overlong."

"I have brought my high-flyer," Brian explained as they walked down the hall. "After this morning's rain, the day has turned out to be very fine." He enjoyed the sight of her blush at the mention of this morning.

They fell silent until they stood before his brother's ridiculously steep phaeton that was painted an eye-catching color of bright yellow.

"Is it safe?" She eyed the high seats with skepticism.

"The courageous Miss Rothwell afraid of a high perch? Surely not," Brian teased. That statement earned him a look of complete disgust.

He smiled.

He did not wish for his ill-timed kiss this morning to result in awkwardness with each other. He valued their friendship. He did not wish to spoil his chances to court her properly once he got the business of the highwaymen done and over. At least then he could act himself instead of parading about like a popinjay.

"Up you go." He helped her climb into the seat.

"Did you purchase this?" she asked. She gripped the sides of her seat as the carriage dipped and swayed when he swung himself up and into the driver's seat.

"Of course not. I am dull, remember? This was my brother's." He snapped the reins, and his matched team of two pulled away from the curb.

"Was your brother a daredevil, then?"

"Indeed. He was up to any manner of mischief

and tomfoolery." Brian lost himself in some not-so-pleasant memories of his brother's haphazard approach to the duties of an heir to Cherring. "I should have been born first," he whispered.

Artemis had heard him, and her eyes grew wide. "Ah, but now you hold the title."

"Yes."

"And you can do with it as you will, just as your brother."

"But I refuse to disgrace it with loose living and rowdy antics." He caught her looking puzzled. He had slipped out of the not-so-serious character he had created for himself. "Pon rep, I bring only an abundance of starched cravats and finery. I ask you, who can find harm in that?"

"I suppose it all depends upon whose opinion you seek."

He wondered if he dared broach the subject of the turn in their relationship. "What if I seek your opinion, Miss Artemis Rothwell?"

She looked taken aback and then thoughtful. "What if I say it is too early for me to completely form one."

"I'd say you are playing it safe indeed. But so be it. I shall not push you for *anything* you are not willing to freely give." There, he thought. That was laced with meaning.

Artemis nodded with some relief. The awkwardness of facing him after this morning's kiss had fallen by the wayside once she got up into the seat of his phaeton and realized he would treat her the same as before. He was still her friend, and although he hinted at wanting something more, he had agreed not to push her. And she had not discouraged him, much to her chagrin.

She decided a change of subject was certainly needed before she said something she would later regret. "Do you think your brother could have done something foolish to the highwaymen that robbed him?"

"I am sure that he did," Cherry answered with tight lips.

"Then perhaps it truly was an accident. His death, I mean."

"Why do you ask?" He turned to look directly into her eyes as if trying to uncover something from her.

"I do not know." But she did. She wanted to gauge the danger of staging a carriage accident. "They took something precious from my family and I want it back. I wish I could catch them myself and take it back."

"So do I," he muttered, his attention back on the crowded roads. "I see our first stop."

Artemis' thoughts tumbled furiously. "Perhaps we should."

"Should what?" He pulled the phaeton close to the sidewalk to park with complete ease.

She felt the seats sway and gripped onto the sides. "Try to catch them. They are rumored to be gentlemen; perhaps they attend the very same functions as you and I!"

Cherry looked more amused than anything else. "You are mad." He jumped down and made his way around to her side.

"I am indeed quite serious. How do we not know that we dine with the very men who stole the Rothwell ring or caused your brother's death?" She saw a spark of something overshadow his normally merry blue eyes. Was it curiosity perhaps? Or even the desire for revenge? The vision of Cherrington with a sword in his hand fighting for real sent a sudden shiver up her spine. "Goodness, there might be any number of unsuspecting females out there being wooed by a criminal. Is it not our duty to do something? Think of that."

"I am desperately trying not to," he drawled as he reached up to help her down.

She ignored his hands. "What if you are one of them?" Artemis teased.

He burst out laughing and put his hands on his hips. "You saw these men. Did any of them dress as fine as I?" He minced about for her inspection.

She dismissed the thought with a giggle.

"Come, Artie, you must confess that you would have noticed the intricate knot of a true gentleman peeking out from under a black coat."

"I suppose you are correct. You are rarely separated from your cravats." Except this morning, she thought. His neck had been a rather strong column for such a slender peacock, she thought as she accepted his aid and slid out of the seat to the sidewalk below, his hands gently at her waist. "Although, one of them was almost as tall as you, and he had blue eyes besides, just as you do."

He leaned toward her. "I am glad that you noticed the color of my eyes," he said with a wicked grin.

She felt hot, cold, and flustered. She stepped out of his light grasp and offered him her arm. "But of course I have. How can I not when you leer at me so."

"Touché."

They entered the first pawnshop with Artemis continuing to argue her point about teaming up to find out the identities of the *gentlemen highwaymen*, as she put it. Brian acted as disconnected and indifferent to the idea as he thought he should. He could have fallen over when she teasingly accused him of being one of them. Luckily, she had only been making fun, and his clandestine activity remained hidden from her.

They visited several pawnbrokers, and each place resulted with the same distressing news—the Rothwell ring had not been brought in. Artemis graciously left her name for the second and sometimes third time. She requested a message be sent to her straightaway the moment they came upon something that matched the description she gave.

Brian wondered if the Leader knew that Artemis searched for the ring. He concluded that he must, since Artemis made no secret of it.

They exited the last shop. Artemis' spirits that had sunk a little with each rejection were low indeed. "Cheer up, Artie. We'll find it somehow."

"That ring has been in my family for generations, and now it is gone."

He squeezed her hand lightly. "Would you like to stop at Gunter's for an ice? It might take the edge off the disappointment."

She looked up and smiled. "That would be quite nice. Perhaps we might discuss ways we can discover the secrets of the highwaymen."

Brian shook his head. "I feel obliged to help you simply to keep you out of trouble. What ideas do you have?" he asked.

"Several, in fact, but let us first share what we know about the gentlemen attending this Season. And do not be such a poor sport. Thanks to you, I can protect myself."

Brian slapped his forehead with the heel of his palm. "What have I done?"

Brian sipped his brandy and paced the floor of his study as he stared at the charts laid out upon the table. He had effectively listed every eligible gentleman who attended this Season and cross-referenced the names of men who regularly called on various ladies during holdups, and still he was no better off than when he had first started.

These men he robbed with may or may not even attend society parties. For all he knew they might stay within the circles of the demimonde. Dressed as he was, he shuttered to think what kind of lewd propositions he might receive if he ventured into that realm of London society.

He sat down at his desk and tried to remember a gesture or mannerism of the highwaymen that he might pair with some of the listed gentlemen. He racked his brain, but could think of nothing. There was so little time to even think when these robberies were executed. He never knew when or where they would happen.

He and Clancy alternately stayed at the flat rented by *John Fellows* often enough to receive the cryptic notes that announced the date and time when they would be picked up by one of the Leader's hired hacks. Clancy had tried repeatedly to follow them, but had yet to succeed. Every other hired hack in London looked too much like another and, needless to say, Clancy lost sight of them. The Leader was indeed clever in keeping the holdup locations completely secret.

He even provided them with mounts once they met up outside of Town. After each crime, instructions were given in order to return the hired horseflesh. But nothing could ever be traced back to the man who had organized them.

Swirling his brandy as his thoughts jumbled into a discouraged mess, Brian ran his fingers through his short hair. There had to be a way to bring these bandits to justice.

Chapter Eight

*T*he next day brought more warm weather, al-though clouds kept the sun from shining. Ar-temis looked out of the window. She held tightly the note she had received from Harriet instructing her to be ready promptly at twelve o'clock for an afternoon of *shopping*. Artemis dashed out of the townhouse when she spied Harriet opening the door of her fami-ly's closed carriage.

"How did you manage to get it?" Artemis asked when she climbed in.

"I told my father that it looked like rain and that I'd need it to keep my packages dry. We truly are going shopping after this so I will not be made a liar."

Artemis frowned when she noticed Harriet's maid in the corner with her needlework.

"Sally will not breathe a word," Harriet told her.

"And neither will you, correct?" Artemis asked her friend.

"And neither shall I."

"Very well, then, let us be off. Does your coachman know where we are headed?"

"I mentioned that I have to run an errand just outside of Town before we visit the shops on Bond Street. He has made no protests." Harriet lifted up a basket of baked goods. "My errand."

"I am sure he will have a choice word or two when we are *stopped*." She experienced nervous doubts about her whole scheme. What if someone was hurt or worse ended like Cherry's brother? Perhaps they should have taken a gig or hired a hack.

She shook her head to clear it. Even Cherry had agreed that perhaps his brother had brought about his own demise with the highwaymen. Artemis wished only to offer a simple trade—three hundred pound notes for the Rothwell ring. She patted her reticule.

Harriet tapped the side of the carriage, and her coachman pulled away into the street. "Where to?" she asked.

Artemis chewed her bottom lip a moment. "We were held up on the northern road just this side of Hampstead. I suppose that is the most logical place to go for a start."

"Very well." Harriet gave directions to her coachman through the trapdoor. Then she turned to Artemis. "What did you tell Miranda?"

"What your note instructed, that I was going shopping with you."

"Good." Harriet settled back in her seat. "No one will expect us for hours."

*   *   *

"Stand and deliver," Brian shouted as he walked out of the woods toward the carriage that sat in the clearing as if waiting for them. He heard giggles that were definitely feminine coming from inside. His fellow bandits came out of the woods as well, and they easily surrounded the carriage that was driven by a decidedly unconcerned coachman.

One of the men took to the roof to tie the coachman's hands. It was an easy task, since the fellow held his hands out in complete surrender.

Brian sighed. This had all been staged. It had been the third one this month.

The Leader opened the carriage door. Three young ladies, wearing jewels dripping from their ears and necks, gingerly descended the steps with silly grins upon their faces.

The Leader lined the ladies up, took their offered baubles in exchange for a kiss that left the flighty fillies practically swooning.

"Oh, please, sir," a tiny brunette pleaded. "Can I not see your face, just this once?"

The Leader played his part well. He bowed deeply before apologizing to the girl. "I am afraid not, *ma petite.*" The French endearment only served to make the young ladies sigh all the more. " 'Tis a dangerous game we lads play, and I fear our adventures must soon come to an end. But I thank you for these." He held up the jewels. He jerked his head for his men to follow and disappear into the woods.

Brian carefully watched each bandit as they scurried away from the road. They stopped to divvy up the loot, and Brian tried to find something that might give him some clue who these men might be. Each wore black greatcoats that hid their build. Kid gloves kept their hands hidden from view, and their hair color was pretty much covered with their hats; the features of their faces concealed with a long black mask. Only the color of each man's eyes could be detected, two sets of brown and one set of blue.

Brian broke the vow of silence when he whispered, "Is it true, are we soon to be finished?"

The Leader glared at him. "Watch your tongue."

When the other men stopped sorting through the fairly common jewelry, some of it made of paste, they looked at the Leader and waited expectantly for an answer.

The Leader sighed. "Sorry, boys, but we cannot go on forever and expect not to get caught. It's too dangerous now with these ladies staging carriage breakdowns and the like to lure us. Can't tell when one might be full of Red Breasts."

The men nodded sullenly. Brian was shocked at the solemn disappointment that settled over them. These men enjoyed this charade far too much. Brian felt a wave of panic that they might slip away to oblivion before he'd have a chance to turn them in.

The Leader stood. "Perhaps we might have a go of it once more. Wait to hear from me." And then he stood and watched the men scatter, as was their routine.

Brian hunched down into a little knoll of grass once he was farther into the woods. He spied the Leader weaving his way through the grove of trees to the left of him. Brian wondered if he might succeed this time if he followed. Creeping around the edge of the clearing to where he thought the Leader had gone, Brian was once again thwarted. The man had effectively disappeared.

Brian uttered an oath under his breath. He was running out of time.

"Artemis, we need to leave," Harriet said again.

Artemis stalked around the carriage once more before dejectedly agreeing. "I know."

"We have sat here for over two hours, and we have yet to shop. My parents will worry if I do not make it back in time for their afternoon tea."

"Perhaps we can return tomorrow," Artemis hinted.

"I do not know. I will be in the suds as it is."

Artemis let out a pent-up breath of frustration. "I do not know what else I can do. Cherry promised to help me find the ring, but there is only so many pawnshops to search."

"Lord Cherrington is helping you?" Harriet asked.

"He said that he would."

"Then perhaps he might bring you out here."

Her friend was in a pother. "Harriet, I am sorry the highwaymen did not come, but what else could I have done. I simply have to come back. Cherry will hardly agree to do this. You are the only one who can help me."

"But I cannot risk my father's wrath, or I'll be sent packing."

"I do not mean to pull caps with you. I thank you for the effort you took to bring me here, but somehow I have to do this again. If not on this road then another."

Harriet lifted the trapdoor to order her coachman to Bond Street for a couple of quick purchases.

Artemis dressed with care, her thoughts on the words of advice from Lord Cherrington. He thought the simplest of gowns looked best on her. She chose to wear a silk gown of the palest green with an overlay of silvery filet lace. The dress felt as cool as it looked and fell simply from the waist to the floor, with no flounces or ribbons. The neckline was a broad square detailed with embroidered silver thread. It barely covered her shoulders, and the tiny, capped sleeves exposed much of her arms, but she felt like a grand fairy queen, since her maid had placed little silvery leaves in her upswept hair.

Well, perhaps a very large fairy indeed, she decided as she looked at her tall length in the mirror. She shrugged. For once she did not quite mind her height.

She dabbed a few drops of Lily of the Valley perfume behind her ears and upon her wrists. She pulled on her delicate sheer white gloves, also embroidered with silver thread that she had purchased just this afternoon.

She breathed deeply in an attempt to calm her jitters. She was as pleased with her appearance as she ever could be, but still she trembled in anticipation of tonight's rout.

"How lovely you look," Miranda said when she peeked into the room.

Artemis turned around. "Do you really think so?"

Miranda opened the door wide and smiled. "I do.

You have come quite a long way from the young lady at the hunting party this past autumn. You have Town polish, my dear, and it becomes you."

Artemis cocked her head. Had she finally grown up, then? She hoped to prove it when her parents came for her by presenting them with the Rothwell ring. She wanted to get it back herself, like the independent woman she knew she had become. The readings of Mary Wolstencraft had taught her to be the author of her own destiny. Perhaps in some small way, she was making strides toward that end.

She arrived at the rout, already a tight squeeze, on the arm of Ashbourne. Miranda was on his other arm. She looked up at him as if he were family and smiled.

"You are doing very well, Miss Rothwell. I hear that several gentlemen left their cards this afternoon while you and Miss Whitlow were shopping."

She felt a tug of guilty conscience, but put it aside. She and Harriet had made quick work of the shops on Bond Street, and Artemis arrived home just in time to receive Lord Cole. She was delighted to have the chance to talk with the young lord alone, but again, she was not thrilled with the conversation. They spoke entirely about horseflesh. Lord Cole had not even bothered to bow or kiss her hand when he took his leave. "Thank you, Ashbourne."

They were not two steps into the main room when Cherry made an excellent leg before them. "Lord Ashbourne, might I take Miss Rothwell off your arm?" he asked with a wink.

Ashbourne's lips curved into a rueful smile as he gave her over. Artemis could tell that Ashbourne was not impressed with the man even though Cherry had dressed rather somberly this evening.

"Come, the refreshments are across the room." Cherry took her hand, threading his fingers through hers.

Her stomach flipped over, and she stopped. "I do not think I want anything just now. I feel a little sick."

Cherry looked concerned. Without warning, he reached out and touched her forehead with the back of his hand.

She hurriedly pushed it aside. "Cherry, think where we are." She looked around to see if anyone had noticed the familiar gesture.

"Look who has become a pattern card of proper behavior," he teased. "What is wrong, is it your head? Perhaps you caught a chill in the rain."

"No. I am fine now." She made a face.

"Hmmmm. Perhaps you need some air." He pulled her along.

She tried to release his hand, but he held fast as they weaved their way through the throng of people out onto the balcony. It was also filled with guests.

Finally he let go of her, and she absently wiped her gloved hand against her skirt. She looked around at the large terrace, decorated with tiny lights hanging from trees that surrounded the balcony. The moon shone full and cast even more soft light upon them. Artemis mused that she stood amid a fairyland with the hum of chatter sounding suspiciously like the rapid beating of wings. She glanced at Cherry, her *Oberon*, and she was at a loss for words.

"Artie," he whispered, "are you sure you are feeling well?"

She shook her head. "Of course I am. I just . . ." Someone bumped her from behind, and she literally fell into his chest. She felt his arms tighten around her, and her stomach flipped over again.

"You look lovely tonight," he said softly, his eyes dark with his black pupils taking over most of the blue.

Her voice sounded strange, as if she were deprived of air. "Thank you. You do too."

"Lord Cherrington, Artemis, there you are." Harriet broke whatever spell had been cast over them.

Artemis pulled quickly away from Cherrington. "Good evening, Harriet."

"Miss Whitlow." Cherry bowed gracefully. Artemis thought she detected a bit of annoyance in his voice.

Harriet looked puzzled. She looked at each one of them in turn. "Oh, those gloves look quite nice with that dress. They are the very thing. I am so glad you purchased them."

Artemis spread her fingers wide as she held out her hands for inspection. "I rather like them."

"Thank goodness we made it back in time for tea, or I would have been deep in the briars."

"Out shopping too long?" Cherry asked.

Artemis tried to make every imaginable expression to keep Harriet from spilling their afternoon adventure, but Cherry caught her. She looked away, guilty.

"Not shopping?" he asked with a cocked brow. "Where were you two ladies this afternoon?"

"We took my father's carriage north of the Hampstead road."

"Harriet," Artemis warned.

"Now, let me guess." Cherry shifted his weight to one foot and flourished his hand dramatically. "You ladies were not perhaps looking for a certain band of highwaymen, now, were you?"

Artemis cast a scathing look toward Harriet, who looked triumphant, as if it was her plan all along to tell him.

"Perhaps you might take her next time, Lord Cherrington. She wants to go back, since the bandits never showed."

"No doubt robbing some other pea-gooses with feathers for brains!" He turned to Artemis. "Why did you not tell me?"

Artemis' defenses rose. "Because you would have found a way to prevent me from going."

"You have that right."

Artemis turned to her friend, who looked ready to skulk away into the shadows. "Harriet, look what you have done."

"She did right," Cherry admonished. "What possessed you to do such a thing? Please do not say you were hoping for a kiss as the other ninnies here this Season."

"I want my family's ring!" Artemis ground out between clenched teeth. "I would never go to such lengths for something as paltry as a kiss."

"Was it not good enough, then?" he asked with a whispered snarl.

"What on earth are you talking about?"

Brian stopped in his tracks. Both ladies were looking at him as if he had grown two heads. Good God, he was acting jealous of himself! "Nothing," he said. "I simply overheard some ladies chatting about

wanting kisses from the highwaymen, and I
assumed . . ."

Artemis looked indignant. Miss Whitlow looked
amused, as if she saw through to the jealousy he felt.

"I think I would like some punch now, if you
please," Artemis said with her nose in the air as if
she had no intention of going with him to fetch it.

He took a deep breath, ready to argue, when he
thought better of it. Distance would definitely clear
his head. Perhaps it was that gown she wore with the
incredible view of her womanly charms, or perhaps it
had suddenly become difficult to breathe when he
was around her. It mattered not. He'd get the punch.
"Miss Whitlow, might I bring a glass back for you?"

"I should like that above all things." Again with
the knowing smile! He could have cheerfully choked
her. She had taken Artemis into a potentially harmful
situation, and he could not banish the thought of
what might have happened. It did not matter that he
would have been there had they been held up.

As he made his way to the punch table, his
thoughts churned in an unwanted direction. Perhaps
Artemis had the right of it after all. What if he could
somehow lure the Highwaymen into a trap? With
Artemis as the bait. He did not like it, but he had to
own that he was running low on options.

"I think he cares for you," Harriet whispered.

"Who?" Artemis knew very well of whom her
friend spoke.

"Lord Cherrington."

Artemis rolled her eyes. "We are but friends. Besides, look at him."

"Oh, pish and fiddle," Harriet sputtered. "You could change all that."

Artemis' eyes narrowed. "How do you mean?"

"I have been told that my father was a hardened rake until my mother got hold of him. She reformed a rake, why can you not reform a tribble?"

Brian returned with the glasses of punch. He had downed two of his own while at the table. He could not get the idea of creating a trap out of his head. Artemis, he mused, would no doubt be willing, since she wanted to return and stage a carriage accident anyway. He could make sure that Clancy went along as her servant.

"Your punch." He offered the ladies their cups.

Miss Whitlow kept glancing between them over the rim of her glass, and Brian wondered just what the ladies had discussed in his absence. Artemis looked flushed, but then hadn't she said that she did not feel well? Perhaps he should offer to take her home early and they could discuss his idea more at length.

The most important thing was her safety. He would, of course, be there. Clancy and the entire force of Runners could also be present. Plus they might have the element of surprise on their side. Surely, it would be all right. It just might work.

"Cherry?" Artemis asked.

"Yes?"

"Thank you for the punch." She glanced at him almost shyly before turning her attention back to Miss Whitlow.

Brian had seen all sorts of feminine wiles applied,

but he swore he had never seen such a flirtatious look from a woman in his life. And he'd bet a monkey she did not even know she had done it. "Feeling better, then?" he asked.

"I believe I am."

"Excuse me," Miss Whitlow said. "I see someone I simply must speak to."

Brian watched Artemis watch her friend walk away from them. She acted nervous, as if she'd been left behind with the wolves. "Tell me what happened today, and perhaps I can help you," he said.

She looked up at him, her eyes wide. "With the carriage?"

"Yes. What did you intend to accomplish by sitting there waiting for the masked men?"

She looked around at the several people near them and hesitated.

He held out his arm. "Would you prefer to walk along the garden path? It is well lit, and see there are other couples taking a stroll, so there can be no harm as long as we remain in full view on the main path." When she chewed her bottom lip as she considered his request, he added, "We shan't be gone overlong."

"Very well." She took his arm, and they walked down the terrace steps toward the garden.

They passed a couple on the path, and Brian caught a raised eyebrow from the lady who had been one of the circle he'd paid court these past weeks. The gentleman, also a member of Boodle's, offered Brian a salacious smirk. Obviously there would be gossip on the morrow.

Brian was determined to remain firmly upon the path and in plain sight at all times, even though he was sorely tempted to pull Artemis onto a hidden bench and have his way with her. Then again, he could not be certain that she would not dash off like a frightened rabbit again.

If her fidgets and silence were any indication of the discomfort she felt, then he'd have a hard time turning this walk into anything romantic. She kept glancing sideways at him as if she did not quite know what to make of him. Those questioning looks warmed his blood considerably.

"Can we talk now?" she whispered.

"Of course."

"Here is my plan to get the ring back," she said. "I would like to offer the highwaymen a trade. I have three hundred pounds. I will give them the funds for the ring."

Brian whistled. "Where did you get such a sum? Surely not your pin money."

She actually laughed softly. "Of course not. My stepmother left it with me in order to purchase the ring back from a pawnbroker."

"I see." Brian rubbed his chin. "Did you have the notes on you when you staged your little accident?"

She turned a defensive glare upon him. "Yes."

Brian stopped walking and faced her. "Artie, what if you truly had been robbed? They would have taken your money and left you with nothing!"

She wrinkled her nose. "I had not thought of that."

"No, I suppose not." He took her arm again and patted her hand. "This time, let me plan our mode of attack. Perhaps we might even lure these fellows into a trap so the Runners can finally bring them to justice."

She stopped walking and turned to face him. "Oh, Cherry, a capital idea! Tell me what you want me to do."

"My, how very eager you are to accept my counsel." He gave her a playful wink. "And I thought I'd have to argue to be the one in charge."

"As long as you continue to make sense, you may make the plans," Artemis said. They resumed walking and passed two more couples.

"Perhaps we should table our discussion until tomorrow morning, then? It will give me some time to think on it."

She nodded.

They heard the sounds of a couple behind a tree. Brian chuckled. "It appears that we have stumbled upon a lovers' tryst. Would you care to return?"

Artemis would not look at him. Even in the dim light, he could imagine how red her cheeks were. "I would like that above all things," she said.

Chapter Nine

*A*rtemis slipped through the boxwood hedge. "Good morning, Cherry."

"Artie." His smile was easy and warm. "I have a surprise for you."

She hurried her steps to meet him under the awning. "What is it?"

"What, no pleasantries, Miss Impatient?" he teased with his usual drawl.

She knocked his shoulder playfully. This was what she liked the most about Cherry. He took nothing too seriously. "Do tell me, or I shall expire from curiosity." She leaned back and draped her hand across her brow with mock melodrama.

He laughed. "Somehow that pose does not suit you." He unrolled a small canvas that held two lethal-looking daggers with intricately carved handles of ivory.

Artemis ran her finger gently over the hilt. She sat down on the bench near the table to better examine the knives. "These are beautiful. Where did you get them?"

"While I was in India," he said.

She looked up at him. "India?"

"Of course. I traveled extensively on the Continent, don't you know." He placed a protective sheath over the blades. "My surprise is that I will teach you to wield a dagger as competently as you flourish a sword."

Artemis' gaze narrowed to make sure he did not jest.

"I have given the idea of luring the highwaymen considerable thought. I want you to carry one of these." He handed her a dagger. "I will show you how to use it."

A chill raced up Artemis' spine. The danger became very real, and for a moment she wanted to change her mind and back out. But the vision of her stepmother humiliated by the Leader of that band of thieves gave her a renewed flush of anger. She wanted the Rothwell ring back where it belonged on her stepmother's finger. If they could bring these men to justice while getting that ring, then so much the better. "How shall we lure them?"

"I think we should place an advertisement in the *Post*; a discreet announcement of sorts with our intent and the time and place given. Then we shall simply have to go there and wait to see if they take the bait. Since we have no clues to their identities, I think this might be the fastest way to catch them."

Artemis nodded.

"Very well." He offered her his hand. "Shall we commence?"

Artemis' fingers tingled at Cherrington's touch, but she shrugged off the feeling. Now certainly was not the time to examine it. She needed all her concentration centered on learning how to fight with a dagger.

But Harriet's words had not left her. Could she reform him? Could she urge Cherry to disregard his outlandish clothes and powder for more manly attire?

Brian was not in the least surprised that Artemis took to the dagger as if she had always used one. She was quick and handled the shorter blade with utmost ease. He showed her how to unsheathe it quickly and then replace it. He said a fervent prayer that she would never need to use it.

After his short demonstration with the dagger, they returned to the fencing lessons. They parried and thrust for nearly an hour until they were both spent and panting. Brian sat down at the table with a groan and reached to pour a glass of lemonade for Artemis. Clancy appeared with a tray of sliced fruit and biscuits, followed by the housekeeper with tea.

Brian nodded to them both, and they returned to the house after leaving the refreshments.

"My goodness, such a spread." Artemis took a slice of apple and popped it into her mouth.

"My desire is your command." He gestured with a flourish.

She burst out laughing.

He loved the sound of her laugh. It was not the practiced little tinkle that so many of the ladies performed to perfection. Artemis expressed real amusement. In fact, everything about her was real and that's what he loved about her. He suddenly stood up.

He loved her!

"Cherry, what is wrong?"

"Uh, nothing. I simply thought of something I must not forget to do." He quickly resumed his seat. He looked at her as the realization of his feelings for her sunk in with something akin to fear. How could she possibly come to feel the same for him when he was not himself?

He should tell her what he had been up to, but knew that he could not. Not yet. It was too risky. He could not be sure of her reaction or how she would behave when they made the trade of money for the Rothwell ring. If she gave up his identity, the whole thing could crash about their ears. And they might not have another chance.

He was jerked out of his revelry when Artemis waved her hand in front of his face. He blinked.

"Are you still with me?" she asked. "You looked miles away."

"I was thinking about our plan," he said.

"You will place an advertisement." She got up and went to the tea cart. "Shall I pour tea?"

"Yes. I shall place the ad today. Wait one moment." Brian reached into the inside pocket of his coat that he had draped across the far end of the table. He pulled out his little notebook and flipped it open, a small piece of charcoal ready. "You were held up on the North Road bound for Hampstead, correct?"

"Yes, about a mile south of the little stone chapel." Artemis grabbed the notebook out of his hands before he could stop her. She fingered through the pages and looked at him in horror. "There is an entire list of gentlemen you think might be potential highwaymen. My goodness, their current financial situation, their reputations—why you even have Lord Cole listed and Mr. Clasby. Neither could be the highwaymen; it is absurd to think so." She shut the book with a little snap. "You have been after these fellows all along, haven't you?"

"Yes," Brian admitted. He reached across and took back his notebook.

"Are you using me to get at them?"

He stared into her eyes. "What if I said that in a way, I was?"

She sat back down on the bench with a slump. She twitched her lips and wrinkled her nose as she thought about what he had said. "Well," she started. "Your brother did die at their hands even if it was an accident and perhaps one caused by his own reck-lessness." She peeked up at him to gauge his reaction to that statement. When he said nothing, she contin-ued. "I suppose you have the right to seek revenge. I wanted to stage more carriage breakdowns regard-less, but how does this help?" She pointed at the notebook.

Brian relaxed. "I have been jotting down my obser-vations about various gentlemen, and yet I have gained nothing. As you so eloquently stated, my list of suspects is vast and quite ridiculous. 'Tis like look-ing for a needle in the proverbial haystack."

"Why did you not stage your own carriage acci-dent?" Artemis asked. "You could have encountered these gentlemen for yourself."

"It did not seem to be a good solution until I heard about what you were trying to do. Offering to pay the bandits for the ring just might lure them in. The

Leader cannot place it for pawn, since you have scoured the shops. A shop owner might tell Bow Street once the Leader turned the thing in."

"Oh. I had not thought of that. By constantly inquiring about the ring, I have made it impossible for the highwaymen to pawn it."

"Something like that," he said.

"Why did you not say something when we paraded to all those pawnbrokers?"

"The damage had already been done. Your visit with me was not your first. Besides, it was enough to spend time in your company." It was absolute truth, and he braced himself for her reaction.

She looked away from him and concentrated on her tea. But her cheeks had colored to a soft pink, and Brian was encouraged.

After a quick sip, she looked up. She looked determined when she said, "We shall succeed, Cherry. You shall have your revenge, and I shall have the Rothwell ring!"

He hoped she had the right of it.

"It has grown late." Artemis set down her cup with a clink upon the marble table. "Will you go to Almack's tonight?"

"Indeed, I will. We shall talk more then."

Artemis got up to head across the lawns and stopped. Turning around, she asked rather shyly, "Might you dress as you did last evening?"

"Why, Artie, I did not think you cared." When she stumbled over her words to make amends for her request, Brian soothed her with a wink. "I will dress as you wish. Like I said, your command is my desire."

He enjoyed watching her falter and smile before she darted toward Lady Ashbourne's townhouse. He rubbed his chin, deep in thought. She wanted him to dress with taste . . .

Artemis looked for Cherry. She spotted him amid his usual circle of ladies, and irritation lanced through her as sharp as a sword's point. Not bothering to bow or scrape to the patronesses of Almack's hallowed halls, Artemis walked straight toward him.

"Ah, Miss Rothwell," he smiled when he saw her, disentangling himself from one of the Waterton-Smythe sisters.

"Lord Cherrington, good evening." Artemis waited.

"Ladies, please excuse me. I have a prior engagement with Miss Rothwell for a dance."

It was all Artemis could do not to stick her tongue out at the ladies when they sighed with disappointment. She did not miss the nasty comment whispered about her gargantuan appearance, but she did not care a whit. Instead of feeling awkward and uncomfortable, she furiously raised her chin at the overheard insult.

Cherry grinned at her when she took his offered arm. "You were indeed subtle, my dear," he said sarcastically.

Artemis felt her back stiffen. "Whatever can you mean?"

"I think the snapping of your fingers would have sent an equally clear message."

Artemis pulled away. "If you wish to return to your, your court of clucking hens, be my guest."

He pulled her back and patted her hand. "Artemis, I am merely teasing you. For a moment, I thought you might actually be jealous." He gave her a sly glance.

Jealous! Artemis was about to refute such a claim, when she realized that was it exactly.

"Trust me," he whispered in her ear causing a delicious shiver. "They care not for me. 'Tis only my title that has them flocking."

"That and your fashion advice." Her voice had softened with a hint of a smile.

"I suppose that too." He led her out onto the dance floor as the music of a waltz lilted in the air. "Might I add that again you have chosen well this evening? That gown is perfect."

Artemis felt a rush of pleasure at his compliment. He too had dressed to please her. He wore a fashionably dark coat that hugged his broad shoulders over an equally dark waistcoat. His knee breeches of black were simple, as were his stockings. His flat pumps bore no buckles or bows. He looked lean and elegant.

She only wished that he had not worn face powder. It gave him such a pallid complexion as if he had been ill. Even his hands looked like he had lightened them. Well, it was a start, she thought.

When his arm encircled her waist and his hand took hers, she melted into Cherry's arms and followed his lead. An excellent dancer, he made her confident of her own steps. When he pulled her closer, she did not demure. In fact, she looked into his merry blue eyes and remained there. He made her feel comfortable and uncomfortable at the same time. With him, she felt completely feminine even though it made no sense considering his infernal primping.

"I have placed the advertisement in the *Post*. It should run in the morning offering to meet the following day."

She felt a surge of panic. "So soon."

"I think that is best. Surprise must remain on our side."

She nodded as they turned and dipped to the music.

"You have seen these highwaymen, is there nothing that you remember that might resemble any of the gentlemen here?" he asked.

Artemis looked about quickly. "It happened so very fast. One man was quite taller than the others, much like your height. But then they all wore generous greatcoats that made it impossible to judge their size. I have seen a couple gentlemen of similar stature, but who could tell if they might have played a bandit. Lord Cole, for instance, is nearly as tall, but I cannot imagine him traipsing about in a mask."

Cherry's voice was a mere whisper. "What about the one who kissed you?"

Artemis gasped. "I never told you that I had been kissed."

"It is their trademark, as it were." His eyes twinkled with mischief.

Artemis felt her cheeks grow warm. "You are teasing me again."

"I like the way your cheeks turn pink. Besides, I am intolerably curious to find out how his compares to mine."

She felt the heat in her cheeks deepen. "As I have

already said, it happened so fast. Perhaps I shall have to invite the tall Highwayman to kiss me again so that I might give you a full report."

"Ah," he said. "You are so sure of mine, then, or do you need another example?"

Artemis did not answer, but her insides felt unstable and her head a little light. Both kisses she received were indeed unforgettable, but she was not about to tell Cherry that she liked his much better.

"Well, Clancy, the wheels are in motion," Brian said as he scrubbed his face. "There is no going back now."

"I'll see to it that she remains safe and sound," Clancy said.

"I know that, else I would not have allowed her to be used as bait."

"I don't see as how I can make a pretty maid, but then you must help me with my costume." Clancy adjusted the loose bodice of a maid's dress.

Brian laughed. Clancy would be no good to anyone if he were tied up. The highwaymen never bothered to tie up female servants. He would send his own coachman to drive with Clancy, who would play Artemis' maid. It should not matter a whit that it was his crested carriage. He was considered Artemis' most serious suitor.

He would alert Bow Street to his plan tomorrow, after reading the *Morning Post* and clarifying the details with Artemis. He wanted no mistakes.

Artemis gathered the coverlet up to her chin as she settled back into plump pillows. She lay staring at the bed's canopy, hoping she and Cherry were not acting out a fool's errand by attempting to catch the highwaymen. A soft knock on the door interrupted her thoughts.

"Come in," she called.

Miranda entered her bedchamber. "In bed so soon? Might we have a coze?"

Artemis sat up and brought her legs underneath her to make room for Miranda to sit down. "Is anything amiss?"

"Heaven's no," Miranda said. "I simply wanted to talk to you."

Artemis waited quietly, and when Miranda hesitated, she urged, "Out with it."

Miranda smiled. "How do you feel about Lord Cherrington?"

"Why?"

"Because Lord Cole paid a call on Evan today. He has asked his permission to offer for your hand."

Artemis felt a fleeting moment of glee followed by dread. "What did Ashbourne say?"

"He cannot make that decision. He informed Lord Cole that your father would return to Town before the Season's end. The matter must be taken up with him. But not before asking you first, of course. It would seem that you have greatly impressed Lord Cole."

Artemis bit her bottom lip. "So it would seem."

"Yet you have often been in the company of Lord Cherrington. I wondered where your preferences lay."

"Oh, dear," Artemis whispered. It was true that she had received several gentlemen callers after balls or parties as expected. But Lord Cole had singled her out. For once in her life, she did care to speak only of horses.

"I thought as much," Miranda said with a smile.

"What?"

"You are smitten with Lord Cherrington."

"How can you tell?"

"You come alive when you see him. A slight blush steals over your cheeks, your eyes sparkle a bit more."

Artemis threw herself against her pillows with a groan. "Papa will never approve of him. Never."

"What does your heart tell you?"

Artemis groaned again. "I wish I knew. Harriet says that I might reform Cherrington's primping ways in time."

"Harriet is correct, you might. But what if you do not? In the end, will it matter to you overly much? If so, he cannot be the one for you."

"Lord Cole certainly is not the one for me." Artemis did not wish to discuss her uncertain feelings for Cherry. She felt ashamed that she did not wish to accept him as he was.

"Lord Cole is a handsome man," Miranda said.

"Yes, but he does not act like I am a female. He talks only of horses and hunting. When he dances, he is stiff as a board. Lord Cole holds me far away while Cherry tends to pull me rather close. . . ." She stopped, horrified that she admitted such a thing to her stepmother's best friend.

Miranda's expression was all too knowing. "You must follow your heart, my dear, and the rest will fall into place. But do be forewarned that Lord Cole might broach the subject with you. I wanted you to be prepared. You must make the right decision for yourself, not for your father's approval."

"Yes, I understand. I cannot possibly jilt another gentleman and get away with it." Artemis smiled. She was indeed grateful that there was no discomfort between them.

Miranda laughed. "No, you cannot or the Waterton-Smythe sisters will positively pull their hair out."

"Now, that would be a sight to see. Perhaps, I should think more on Lord Cole's offer."

"Do not dare," Miranda scolded before leaning over her to kiss the top of her head. "Have a good night's sleep, my dear, and sweet dreams."

Artemis yawned and snuggled under the covers after Miranda left her room. Her advice had always been sound. She now knew that she should never settle for simply a comfortable marriage. She would rather remain unwed. If it came to that, she needn't marry if she did not wish to. The idea that Lord Cole might offer for her did not tempt her in the least. Nor did Mr. Mellowby or Lord Ranton or any other gentleman she had met this Season.

Only with the thought of spending time in the arms of Lord Cherrington did she experience that odd flip of her insides, followed by warmth all over. But could she come to terms with his appearance? And as Miranda had hinted, it was not fair to view him with such discrimination. Artemis knew too well what it was like not to be accepted. She had received her own good measure of disapproving glares to last a lifetime.

Chapter Ten

*H*e took a sip of his tea and flipped open the *Morning Post*. He sat straighter in his chair when he read an advertisement posted halfway down the page near the society news. He read it again.

> To the Leader of Bandits who took an heirloom, I wish to make an exchange worth your time and effort at the very same place and same time as before on the morrow. I am certain that you know who makes this request. I shall not bring a pistol.

He set the paper down with a smile curving his lips. Miss Rothwell wished to make a trade. She must have finally tired of haunting the pawnshops.

The time to end his escapades had come. His cohorts could easily be delivered to the Runners in order to ruin them. The taste of revenge promised incredible sweetness.

Miss Rothwell's invitation might very well be a trap, but then it mattered not. He knew he played a dangerous game. Answering the advertisement gave him the very opportunity he had been considering. He would be fully prepared in order to get away without anyone the wiser—without getting caught.

He leaned back in his chair and folded his hands behind his head. This might be just what he needed to get even on all accounts. He would turn in his men as he had planned, and somehow he would find a way to ruin Artemis Rothwell in the process.

"Did you read the *Morning Post*?" Artemis shoved the paper under Cherry's nose. She pointed to the advertisement.

"I placed it, remember?" He cocked one eyebrow.

Artemis let out an agitated sigh and paced. "What if he does not know who is requesting the trade? I am sure there must be any number of heirlooms stolen."

Cherry stood directly in her path. He placed both of his hands upon her shoulders to still her. "Trust me, he knows. I mentioned a pistol to clinch it for him. I am certain that you are the only female who has pulled a gun on him. Besides, I had to be discreet or Lady Ashbourne would no doubt suspect."

Artemis wrinkled her nose. "I suppose you are correct. How did you know about the pistol?" Perhaps it was nerves that plagued her to the point of being irritable. She had never mentioned it to anyone.

Cherry cocked his head as if thinking. "Did you not tell me?"

Artemis narrowed her eyes. "I have told no one. Not even Harriet."

"Perhaps, then, it was your stepmother, or Lady Ashbourne. They are quite proud of you, you know."

It would be just like Miranda to boast to Cherry. She rather thought that Miranda favored him from the start. Considering that he had saved her reputation on more than one occasion, he could not have been surprised by the news of her actions. And it had been clever of him to word the advertisement in such a manner as to distinguish her without giving away her identity.

Even so, she had taken every copy of the *Morning Post* from the townhouse to be safe. No one could possibly know what she was about to do. "I suppose you have the right of it."

"Of course I do." He draped one arm around her shoulders and steered her back to the marble table under the awning. "I have ordered my coffee out-of-doors, since we are meeting so early; you must join me."

Artemis followed and sat down. He poured a cup of fragrantly steaming brew for her and one for himself. She added milk and sugar. Cherry drank his black. "Is it not bitter to drink it that way?" she asked.

"Not at all. This is a fine blend." He raised his cup as if in a toast. "One of the advantages of trade with the East India Company. I brought it back with me when I was in India."

Artemis took a sip. It was stronger than she was used to, but definitely smooth. She helped herself to a biscuit from the tray and bit into it, chewing quickly. "What brought you to India? That must have been quite an extension of your Grand Tour."

"I had business there."

"Tell me about it." Artemis relaxed, ready for a

story. She did not want to think about tomorrow, nor did she wish practice at swords just yet. She simply wanted to enjoy the delicious coffee and listen.

" 'Tis an interesting country really. There are the very rich and the very poor, much like England and yet so different in every other way. I entered into a partnership with an army officer who had sold out his commission but had married an Indian woman who did not wish to leave her family. We dealt in spices and coffees." He raised his cup. "We had several contracts with the East India Company."

Her eyes grew wide. She was indeed impressed. "I had no idea. I thought you simply traveled the continent like a tourist. You are full of surprises, Lord Cherrington. I do believe there is more to you than fashion and fripperies."

He made a mock bow with his head. "Of course, my dear. Just as there is so much more to you besides your skill at arrows, swords, and horses."

Artemis laughed. "And you have not seen me truly ride."

"And what would you call Rotten Row?"

"Merely a walk in the park. Sissy, my mare, is vexed with me, you know. I spend more time with you than riding. I have neglected her, and she is quite on the high ropes. I do not believe she cares much for London and wants desperately to go home." No one had ever pulled her so completely away from her horse before.

"And what of you? Do you long for home?"

Contemplating her home, she felt an odd sense of loss. She realized that she did not wish to return to Rothwell Park alone. Her life had been rather dull before coming to London. She rather thought she would miss Cherry dearly.

"Perhaps we might make it up to your mare. After our exploits, we must go for a *real* ride."

"I would like that." Artemis looked deep into his merry blue eyes. He did not look away.

"What else would you like, Artie?" he whispered, all merriment gone in an instant.

Flashes of Cherry's kisses flittered through her thoughts, causing Artemis to flush with warmth. Needing a diversion from their course of conversation that was bound to wander onto dangerous ground, she remembered their plan. "I want the Rothwell ring back where it belongs."

She was almost sorry when he became businesslike in a trice. "Well then, let us go over everything once more," he said.

"I think I have it," Artemis said concentrating on the table. "Your man, Clancy, will pose as my maid. I shall take your carriage, driven by your coachman, and simply wait for the highwaymen." She looked up at him. "I will feel the ring in my hand before telling the bandits where the money is hidden in the carriage. I will not carry it on my person or in my reticule."

"Correct."

"And hopefully the Runners will surround us, and no one will be hurt. Who should inform them of what we are doing? I have already spoken to them about the theft; perhaps I should send them a note or some such."

"I shall handle that this afternoon," Cherry said.

She nodded. "Where will you be? In the carriage with me?" she asked with hope in her voice.

He looked away. "No, my dearest Artie. I will remain with the Runners."

Artemis bit her lip. She would feel much better if he would accompany her. "Yes, of course. I forgot."

Cherry stood, then came around the table to kneel beside her. He grabbed both her hands with his own and coaxed her to face him. "Do not worry. Clancy is as adept with the sword as I. He will be well armed, both in pistol and point, I assure you. I will not be far away from you. If anything should happen, you will be my first concern. I promise upon my brother's death, you will come to no harm."

Artemis swallowed hard. She believed him fully. She trusted Cherry with her very life.

Brian saw the worry edge its way out of her gaze, and he was glad for it. He longed to tell her why he could not be in the carriage with her. Escorting the Bow Street Runners seemed like such a lame excuse. For her own safety and his, she could not know that he was one of the highwaymen less she give it away and somehow alert the Leader that they had planned a trap.

He reached out and brushed a stray lock of her dark brown hair off of her forehead. "Do you feel comfortable with how to use the dagger? We could go over it again."

"That is quite all right. I believe I have it."

"Indeed," he said. "Tomorrow morning I have some business to attend to, and then I must go to the Runners' office. Tonight, I must make certain all is set for tomorrow. I shall not see you. Remember to meet Clancy here at half past twelve. You must leave by one o'clock in order to make it to the meeting place with time to spare. Now, what will you tell Lady Ashbourne?"

"She and Ashbourne attend a luncheon tomorrow. They will be gone for hours. I shall leave them a note that I have gone to scour the pawnshops with you and that we took your carriage."

"Very well." He held out his hand as he stood. "Shall we play at swords, then?"

"Indeed." Her hand was warm and soft as she placed it trustingly in his.

They practiced for nearly half of an hour, and Brian felt satisfied that Artemis was proficient. "Here." He handed her the belt and scabbard for the dagger after they had returned to the table under the awning for refreshment. "Wear this tomorrow so that you have fast access to it, if needed."

She nodded, but the fear was back into her eyes, and he wondered if he was doing the right thing. He hated the idea of Artemis feeling afraid. He knew Clancy would protect her, and that gave him some peace. He and Clancy had been through various dangers with pirates when they had sailed with a crew of the East India Company.

Brian, being a single man, was not opposed to such trips in order to inspect their purchases directly before making arrangements for their shipment. He found over the years that personally escorting their most valuable cargo often saved them losses and expenditures in the end.

He peeked at his watch that hung from his waistcoat pocket. It was nearing nine o'clock. "Artemis, you must go, love."

She sighed. "I know." Still, she hesitated to leave.

Brian gave her a lopsided grin. "Much as I would love to, I cannot invite you in, you know."

She smiled and her cheeks turned that delightful shade of pink that was unique only to her. "Just promise me that you will be careful," she said.

He struck a pose and tried for amusement to lighten their moods. "Well, pon rep, you are worried for me."

Artemis did not laugh. Instead she grabbed hold of his waistcoat into her fists and pulled him close to her. "Of course I worry for you, Cherry. You are my dearest friend, my own . . ."

His arms came around her. "Your own what?"

She buried her face into the folds of the cravat he wore, and he melted. He pulled her close and kissed the top of her head, rubbing her back to soothe her. "Nothing will happen to me. Believe it or not, I am quite capable of dealing with this sort of thing."

"Really?" she asked with a muffled voice.

"What if I told you I once clashed swords with a pirate?"

"You must be joking."

"I am not. I helped defend an expensive shipment from thieves. These paltry highwaymen are no matches for me." He had the pleasure of hearing her giggle. He pulled back from her and lifted her chin with his finger. "You will be brave, *oui*?"

"*Oui.*"

He meant to put her from him, but she had other plans. Her hands moved from his waist to his face.

"I wonder what you are hiding under all this powder," she whispered.

"If you wish to know," he said, trapped by her gaze. "I will show you, but not now. You linger too late as it is."

"But I wish to see you as you really are, not so pale." She pulled his already close face to her own.

Her lips were sweet with a hint of coffee still on her tongue when he explored her mouth. There was no reluctance in her this time, and she kissed him with a fervor he felt down to the soles of his feet. Quick in everything he had taught her, kissing was no different. She followed his lead.

Her fingers made mayhem with his hair, but he did not care as he pulled the tie of her long braid loose. He threaded his fingers through the loosened cord and twisted his hands in the silky lengths of her rich brown tresses.

He moaned when he felt her fingers under his shirt, stroking his bare back. He had to put a stop to this, or he was bound to scoop her up and carry her to his bedchamber. "Artemis, please," he groaned. He grabbed her arms to push her away and get her hands off his skin.

She kissed him quickly once more, softly, her eyes open and dreamy looking. And then she stepped back.

He grinned. He could not help it as he looked at her. Bits of the white rice powder had rubbed off onto her face. He wiped a streak of it away and chuckled.

"Kissing is not funny, Cherry," she said, looking self-conscious.

"Of course it is. Even so, I loved it all the same. We can now add *that* to your list of expertise."

She rolled her eyes.

"You must leave, my love, or I shall be sorely tempted to pretend I am not a gentleman." He had the gratification of watching her eyes go wide.

"Yes, of course." She quickly ran her finger down the side of his face. "Your skin is rather dark under there."

"India," he said. "And all that time on ships. It has faded some."

"Is that the reason for the powder?" Artemis asked.

"A gentleman cannot look too leathery, my dear. I have washed with Strawberry water and doused my face with Oil of Talc, but the powder was the only way to lighten my skin evenly." He cocked his head in a mock bow.

Artemis shook her head in amusement. He treated his face more delicately than she had ever done. She looked into his eyes as if realizing something for the first time, but she only whispered with a slight catch to her voice. "Please be careful."

He took her hand and kissed the tips of her fingers. "I promise. You must do the same. Now, please go."

She left, running as she normally did across his lawn. Midway, she turned and cast him a saucy glance that boiled his already heated blood and made him quite literally weak in the knees. "Well, fancy that," he said under his breath. She would no doubt learn to become an expert at other things too.

Brian washed and changed his clothes. As he stood before the mirror, carefully applying a light layer of face powder, he wondered what Artemis must think of him. She obviously had seen past his exterior appearance to the man beneath and that warmed his heart. He wanted so badly to reveal everything about himself, but knew he had plenty of time for that. There was no need to rush Artemis Rothwell. She could make her own decisions, and Brian respected that.

"Your coat, my lord." Clancy helped him slip into the tight-fitting Weston of dark blue superfine.

"Thank you, Clancy," he said, almost as an afterthought. His mind kept running over the scheduled holdup, his insides tense. He would not rest easy till the whole thing was done and over.

"Don't worry, my lord. I'll make sure that your lady is kept safe tomorrow."

Brian turned to face his trusted servant, who was more of a friend. "I know you will. It is just that if anything should happen, I'll never forgive myself."

"We'll just have to see to it that it doesn't."

Brian nodded, his high shirt points making it difficult to turn his head without poking his eyes with the stiffly starched material. "Let us just hope the Runners will be as careful." He made his way out into the hall. "I shall return for dinner, then I believe I should stay the night in Cheapside in case the Leader decides to fetch me early."

"Very good. Would you like me to accompany you?"

"No. Stay here in case Artemis needs you. If anything in the plan changes after I have gone . . ." Brian hesitated a moment. "I will rely on you to handle it."

"Of course."

"Thank you, Clancy," Brian said with deep sincerity. "As usual, you rise to the occasion of each adventure I force upon you, be it good or bad."

"Not at all, sir." Clancy looked a little uncomfortable with the display of gratitude.

"Even so, I thank you all the same."

Brian stepped into the late April sunshine with a terrible weight of responsibility for the success of tomorrow's plan on his shoulders. He not only considered the safety of Artemis and Clancy, but the Runners as well. He had orchestrated the entire scheme, and he hoped to God it did not fail.

He wondered if this heavy feeling was what caused Charles to act out as he did. After their father had died, Charles had become solely responsible for the care of the Cherrington estate and properties. But he had been born to it, and trained for that position, Brian thought ruthlessly. He could not bring himself to excuse his brother's poor behavior simply because it was uncomfortable to be responsible for so many.

He did, however, have a closer understanding for why Charles used the fictitious name of John Fellows in Cheapside to escape his lofty title. Regardless, it was difficult to forgive his late brother for using his alter ego to shirk his duties. Charles should have known better than that. He owed their father more than that.

He took a deep breath when he arrived at the Bow Street Office without paying attention how he had gotten there. He opened the door and went in.

"John Stafford, if you please," he said when a short little clerk raised his head up from his work.

"Who can I say is calling?" The little clerk gave him an insolent look.

"Lord Cherrington." Brian hated to wait, but since there was considerable activity in the office, he cooled his impatience as best he could.

After some ten minutes had passed, John Stafford walked out of his office. "Lord Cherrington, come in, please."

Brian entered the smallish office. "I have a development that will require every man you have tomorrow," he said before he even sat down.

John Stafford cocked a brow. "A trap to capture the highwaymen on the North Road to Hampstead?" He gestured toward the chair.

Brian tilted his head. "How did you know?"

"A letter came only moments ago. The parchment is fine and elegant but with no return information of the sender."

"Ah." Brian relaxed. Artemis had sent the letter. She was nervous about tomorrow as it was, and perhaps it helped her to do something about warning Bow Street on her own. "Might I read it?"

"Of course." Stafford handed it over.

"Short and to the point," Brian said. That was Artemis, certainly, but he was surprised at the soft flowing hand. He had thought her handwriting would be bold strokes to match her personality. He shrugged his shoulders.

"So you believe these men will take the bait of an invitation of pounds for jewels."

"At the last holdup, staged by three young ladies, the Leader mentioned that he wanted to end it soon. That it was becoming too risky."

"What makes you think he will show tomorrow?" Stafford leaned back in his chair.

"Somehow, I know. I think he was furious that Artemis Rothwell had pulled a pistol on him. Plus she has made it nearly impossible for him to pawn the Rothwell ring. Trust me, he will be there. Besides, it is the only chance we have at the moment."

"You make a valid argument. I will have my men placed near the North Road."

"Keep them completely out of sight, or he'll know the jig is up," Brian warned. "And please, no gunfire until I can get Miss Rothwell safely away. I will wear a red rose pinned to my coat so that you will know who I am."

"Won't that look odd to the Leader?" Stafford asked.

"I shall explain that I wear it to give to Miss Rothwell. I was the one to kiss her when we held up her carriage."

John Stafford's face split into a wide grin. "And I will wager you quite enjoyed it."

Brian smiled but remained quiet. It was not something a gentleman bandied about. He returned to the business at hand. "Let me give you the details of my carriage and who will be with Miss Rothwell. I want every possible contingency planned for."

"Of course. We want these man captured without injury. We're hoping to have as much of the loot returned as possible."

Brian did not care about the items stolen, nor did he truly care what injury befell the highwaymen. He wanted them brought to justice—but even more than that, he wanted Artemis kept safe.

Chapter Eleven

*A*rtemis woke late. It had taken considerable time and effort to fall asleep the previous evening. Her maid helped her wash, styled her hair, and then helped her to dress.

Artemis chose a simple morning gown of white organdy muslin with an underskirt of lemon yellow mull. The dress was light and comfortable and gave her the ease of movement she hoped she would not need. Her gaze strayed to the dagger with its small scabbard setting on her desk.

She peeked out of her bedchamber window toward Cherry's townhouse. Had he left for Bow Street? She experienced the now familiar little flip of her insides when she suddenly thought of him and realized she felt far more for him than mere friendship.

Somehow she had to make her father see past Lord Cherrington's foppish ways to the incredibly honorable man that lay beneath. There was no use in denying what she felt for the town dandy any longer. Her decision was made. She wanted to become Cherry's wife.

"Lady Cherrington . . ." she whispered. It sounded so good to her ears. She would let Cherry know her feelings once they finished their business with the highwaymen.

She stepped away from the window and breathed deeply to calm her nerves. What if they did not bring the highwaymen to justice, what then? They had to retrieve the Rothwell ring. It might be the very thing that swayed her father's opinion of Cherry.

Perhaps once her father knew Cherry's part in getting back the Rothwell ring and how he had instructed her to use a dagger and sword, her father would agree to give his permission for Cherry to offer for her.

She knew her father might very well have another reaction. Her family might think what she and Cherry attempted was sheer folly. Her father might rail at Cherry for putting her at risk. But in the end, her family must see that Lord Cherrington treated her with respect and trust.

Cherry thought her capable of the undertaking ahead of them. Although he had teased that he used her, she was more than willing. And was it not her duty as the daughter of a peer to intervene and perhaps stop the highwaymen, given the chance?

She pushed all doubts aside. She was convinced they did the right thing. Clancy would be beside her the whole time. Cherry would be with the Runners, overseeing the entire exchange. She need not fear. She would not be alone, and that gave her considerable comfort.

She smiled when her thoughts returned to the new feelings budding in her heart. She had never before felt so comfortable with a gentleman. Cherry accepted her. He did not attempt to change her into something she was not, nor did he demand more from her than she was willing to give.

She picked up her reticule and stuffed the dagger and its protective scabbard inside. A prick of guilt nagged at her conscience. She hoped to change his appearance, and that could not be fair. She decided there and then that she would not reform him of his outlandish fashion and face powder. Those things did not define the man. She would no longer let them get in the way.

With that settled, she made her way downstairs to the dining room. Miranda and Ashbourne were already seated, enjoying their breakfast. Since meeting Cherry each morning, it had been an age since she had joined them.

"Ah, the lady joins us," Ashbourne said with a smile.

"We did not wake you, did we dear?" Miranda asked as she poured herself a cup of steaming chocolate.

"Not at all. I could not remain a slug in bed when the sun shines so brightly." Artemis helped herself to buttered eggs and thick-sliced ham. She poured herself coffee after she had sat down, dousing it with milk and sugar. She ate in a comfortable silence as Ashbourne and Miranda both read different portions of the current *Morning Post*.

She relaxed. She hoped they had never read yesterday's after she had taken every copy. Neither had mentioned the advertisement Cherry had placed. She sipped her coffee. It tasted good, but it was nothing compared to the aromatic strength of the coffee she had shared with Cherry.

She remembered their kiss, and heat washed over her. She would have no other man, not after yesterday. And she would face Lord Cole with resolve if necessary. But, she needed support in her corner when she did confront her father with her choice at the end of the Season.

Artemis reached across the table for toast, and without preamble, she asked, "Do you think Father might consider Lord Cherrington a worthy suitor?"

Ashbourne's eyebrows lifted toward his hairline, and he glanced quickly at his wife.

"He will," Miranda answered calmly. "Once he sees you with him."

"Do you really think so?" Artemis asked.

"You have a newly acquired softness that suits you well. Your confidence has increased tenfold, and I believe we have Lord Cherrington to thank for that. Sometimes love does that to a person—it brings out all the best."

Artemis looked at Ashbourne. "What are your thoughts?"

He did not appear comfortable with the question. "Your father wishes only for your happiness. If you want Lord Cherrington, then I do not believe Rothwell will gainsay it." He leaned back in his chair. "He may need some convincing perhaps by getting to know the man. By all accounts Cherrington is an honorable fellow. Your father will no doubt see that in time."

"Cherry does not hunt. He has never been to the Quorn or even the Belvoir," Artemis informed them. "And Somerset is a long way from Leicestershire."

Miranda and her husband exchanged amused glances. "You have given this considerable thought, as you should," Miranda said. "The bottom line is simply this—how do you feel about the man? Do you love him?"

Artemis set her knife down, her toast momentarily forgotten. With complete clarity, she knew that she did. "Yes."

"Then there is your answer," Miranda said.

"Indeed," Ashbourne contributed, but he looked as though he preferred to be left out of it. Clearly, he did not think Cherrington the right man for her. Ashbourne had much in common with her father. In fact, the two were so very alike that she feared her father might hold the same opinion.

Brian paced the flat in Cheapside, morning light streaming through the less than spotless windows. He had spent the night and had left only for a few moments to fetch something to eat to break his fast. Everything had been set in motion, and there was no going back now.

Bow Street knew what to do, but even so, Brian felt edgy. Every sound outside his door made him jump, wondering if the Leader's errand boy had come. And then the noise would fade, and quiet invaded the small apartment once again.

He checked his watch. It was nearly twelve o'clock. Artemis would soon meet Clancy. He sat down and drummed his fingers upon the table, waiting. In no time he stood and peered out of the window. He was never any good at waiting. Patience was something he carried in short supply.

Finally a knock at the door drew his immediate attention. He opened it to find a small climbing boy standing on the threshold.

"Yer ride's 'ere govna," the boy said before darting back down the stairs he had just come up.

Brian grabbed his things. The Leader had taken the bait, and the show was about to begin.

Artemis sat in Cherry's carriage across from Clancy, who wore a wig and had dressed like a maid. "Do you think they will show?"

"I do, Miss Rothwell."

"Did Lord Cherrington help you with your costume?" Artemis asked, hoping to pass the time.

Clancy's serious face split into a grin. "Indeed he did, miss. He applied some of his powder to my face, but the rest we managed to scrounge out of the attics."

"You did very well." She peered out of the carriage window again, then checked the tiny watch pinned to just below her shoulder. It was nearly two o'clock. They had been held up shortly before this time, she was sure of it. She could not see a single Bow Street Runner. She hoped they were indeed out there, Cherry among them. "Oh, where are they?"

"They'll be along soon enough." Clancy peeked out of his window too.

"But what if they do not show? What if the highwaymen never read the advertisement, what then? This will all be for naught."

"Let us just sit tight for a few moments more," Clancy said, but his lips had thinned into a tight line of tension.

Artemis could not *sit* in the carriage any longer. "I am going to step out." She did not think it mattered whether she remained in the carriage or stood outside of it. She had invited the highwaymen to come to her.

"I will come with you." Clancy followed her out.

She stretched her arms up high over her head, enjoying the warmth of the sun shining upon her upturned face. She let her arms swing down beyond her sides before placing them on her hips. The scabbard holding the ivory-handled dagger Cherry had given her rested low along the right side of her skirt.

She patted it with her mittened hand and thought better of wearing the lacy gloves. She needed her hands free of any encumbrances. She slipped the mittens off each hand and thrust them into her pockets. She turned and looked at the carriage with its door left wide open. The pound notes her stepmother had given her were hidden deep within a basket of baked goods resting on the seat.

Clancy spoke to the coachman with a low voice. He gave him last-minute instructions to pull away once she was safely inside the carriage after exchanging for the ring.

All she could do is wait.

She looked up and down the North Road leading to Hampstead. There had not been a single traveler for upwards of an hour. A soft wind stirred the nearby trees and ruffled the long grass that swayed this way and that. The swish of the horses' tails at a buzzing fly was the only other noise she heard. The songbirds were quiet. In fact, it seemed entirely too quiet.

Artemis wondered if Cherry and the Runners were even now hiding among those tall trees waiting to catch the masked bandits when they arrived. Knowing that Cherry was out there made her feel safe, but even so, her hand automatically encircled the hilt of her dagger.

The snap of a stick breaking made her tense. She was ready. A heady feeling of anticipation assaulted her senses, and she could not deny that the thought of seeing the tall Highwayman once again pleased her. He had not lived up to his promise, and she relished the chance to remind him of his failure to return the Rothwell ring to her.

In mere moments four men dressed in black greatcoats appeared quite literally from thin air. They stood before her, their black masks hiding every expression they made.

"I have come as you asked, mademoiselle." The Leader stepped forward with a mock bow. He motioned to his men to take their positions. His eyes widened when his gaze connected with the leather belt and scabbard cradling her dagger. "You promised to come unarmed."

"I promised only that I would not bring a pistol," Artemis informed him. Something about the Leader was terribly familiar, but she could not place his voice. His eyes were a common enough shade of brown. She glanced at the other three men. The tall man's back was disappointedly toward her.

"Well then. Let us not tarry longer than needed.

You know why I have come. How much have you brought?"

"First, you must show me the ring," Artemis said.

The other two men walked toward her.

She fingered her dagger, ready to use it. One of the men jumped atop the carriage to tie the coachman while the other man peeked inside.

"Clear," he said gruffly. "It appears that she travels with only her servants."

"Tie her up as well." The Leader pointed at Clancy.

Artemis cast him a panicked glance. This was not supposed to happen. They had not bothered to tie up Marna when she and her stepmother were first held up. She swallowed hard.

Clancy nodded his encouragement even as the Highwayman laced his hands tightly together.

"I am happy to own your *heirloom*," the Leader bragged. "Tell me how much you have brought, or I shall simply walk away." His eyes glimmered ominously. He enjoyed this charade far more than what could be considered natural. The scoundrel had no doubt done this far too often, since he did not act in the least nervous. In fact, he appeared as though he could barely contain his excitement.

"I have two hundred pound notes," she said. "But I am not about to show them to you until I have my family's ring safely in my hand." She extended her hand palm up, and waited.

Brian turned to peek at Artemis, when the Leader whistled at the amount she had brought. She stood tall and proud with her hand insolently stretched out for the ring. The Runners were not supposed to act until after the exchange had been made and Artemis was safely in the carriage.

He was relieved that Clancy's appearance had not raised any suspicion. Their dress rehearsal last evening had proved valuable indeed. After teaching him how to apply face powder to lighten his face and lamp black to darken his lashes, Clancy had passed for a lady's maid, if a bit sturdy of build. He did not like the idea that his hands had been tied. Even so, he knew Clancy was working the knot loose. He was confident in that.

He returned his attention to the trees. They were out there. Bow Street Runners lay hidden in wait for an ambush. Brian stopped twitching his leg. It would do no good to let on how nervous he felt. He wanted nothing of his demeanor to alert the Leader or the other men that this was a trap. He had cautiously explained the red rose he wore to the group's satisfaction, but he could not help but wonder if the Leader had believed him.

Artemis stared at the Leader, daring him to back down from her. She wanted that ring, and she would indeed pay for it as promised. She was a woman of her word. It did not matter that the men would then be caught and the funds returned to her. She would keep her end of the bargain that had been advertised.

She longed to glance into the woods hoping for a glimpse of Cherry to give her confidence, but she knew that she dared not give any indication that she was not alone save the servants that attended her. She kept her gaze steady and willed herself to remain calm.

"Romeo, are we still clear?" the Leader called to the tall man.

"We are." The voice was deep and refined. She wondered if she had ever heard it before, but could not be certain. The thought that she might have danced with these men or that they had called upon her for tea made her shiver. They were indeed gentlemen, and she was in a pucker to find out their identities at last.

With the coachman and Clancy safely tied, the other two bandits stood watch as well, scanning the woods and road. The Leader stepped closer to her. Artemis resisted the urge to step back. He pulled a velvet bag from beneath his coat and handed it to her.

She opened the drawstrings and emptied the contents into her palm. The Rothwell ring, resplendent with diamonds and rubies, glittered in the afternoon sun. She placed the ring on her finger, inspecting it again. Its brilliance could not have been copied. This was indeed the original.

"It is the real article. Trust me," the Leader said. "I could hardly have had one made of paste that would shimmer so well."

Artemis nodded.

"Romeo," the Leader barked, "fetch the pound notes, if you please, and bestow your gift."

The tall man approached her; his mask had fallen low, covering his eyes almost completely. He stopped directly in front of her, but would not look at her. A red rose was pinned to his greatcoat, and he quickly unfastened it. He held it out to her. "As promised, the ring is returned," he whispered. "Please accept this token of my appreciation of your fortitude."

"No thanks to you," she hissed and knocked the rose from his hand. She backed up against the side of the carriage. "Please untie my maid so that she might fetch the money," she ordered.

The tall Highwayman glanced at the Leader for approval.

"Sorry, my giantess, but that maid looks too much like a man. I know some females are decidedly masculine in their appearance. Why, look at you for instance. Your maid stays tied. Tell Romeo of the rejected rose where your pounds are kept."

Artemis fumed. How dare he insult her! She glanced at the bandit called Romeo. His mask did not cover the lower half of his face, and his skin was rather dark. She watched as his jaw flexed and tightened and his lips drew together with obvious displeasure.

"Inside the basket on the seat, underneath the loaves of bread, there is a cloth bag with the funds promised." Artemis glared at the Leader.

Romeo stepped into the carriage as ordered and fetched the pound notes. He jumped down and started for the Leader, bag dangling from his grip.

"No," the Leader stopped him with his hand raised high. "I believe I should like Miss Rothwell to bring my ransom," he drawled.

Artemis felt her blood run cold until ice thickened her veins. The Leader had moved away from them while the tall man retrieved the bag of money. The Leader stood yards away yet it might as well have been miles. She did not want to walk so far away from the carriage. She had promised Cherry to stay close to the carriage. The Leader held his hand open as she had, a challenge in his eyes as he waited.

"You have three hundred pound notes, what else could you possibly want from me," she said, her voice cracking.

"Why, a kiss, of course," the Leader's gaze did not leave her own. "Since you refuse our dear Romeo's rose, perhaps I might have a chance to win your favor."

She looked at Clancy still struggling with the tethers that anchored his hands. He jerked his head toward the carriage. She looked at the open door. The tall man stood next to her and that placed him directly in her way of diving into the opened door. She licked her now dry lips. Perspiration trickled down her back. If she had any kind of chance to throw herself into the carriage, it was now or never.

It happened in a blur. The tall man grabbed hold of her middle just as she pulled out her dagger. She could not hear what the devil he whispered near her ear, since the Leader shouted for him to let her go.

Her heart pounded in her chest, but she did as Cherry had taught her. She thrust her dagger backward. She knew she had connected with flesh when she felt the warmth of blood run over her fingers.

"Artemis," groaned the tall man before he loosened his hold and fell to the ground.

She swayed away from him but not without pulling out her dagger. Frantic, she looked about and saw the Runners coming out of the woods, their pistols drawn. But they were too far away. She had to get into the carriage!

Clancy, hands still tied, bolted for her. She reached out to him, but the Leader suddenly grabbed her with one arm, casting off her balance. With his other hand he knocked Clancy unconscious with a swift blow to the head from the butt of his pistol.

"Let me go," Artemis struggled.

The Leader holstered his weapon and then twisted her arm so that he could take her dagger. He pulled her into his chest and rested the bloodied blade against her neck. "Back off or I'll slit the wench's throat," he yelled at the oncoming Bow Street Runners.

Artemis' knees buckled beneath her. Stars formed and swirled around the edges of her vision. The tall man still lay on the ground. The two remaining highwaymen were caught.

The Leader kicked the bag of pound notes away from the tall man and farther away from the carriage. "We bend down together, or I swear, you'll bleed."

She bent with him.

"Now, pick it up," he hissed.

She did what she was told, the dagger's blade pressed hard against her skin. When they righted themselves, she gazed helplessly at the Bow Street Runners, who stood motionless. There were at least ten of them all told, but they could do nothing. Swallowing her panic, she searched among them, but she did not see Cherry.

Brian came to and swore as pain shot through his leg and groin area. Nausea washed over him when he raised his head, but he had to look. Artemis had used her weapon well. He breathed a sigh of relief as Clancy hovered over him. She had missed his vital organs needed to produce an heir by only four tiny inches.

"Where's Artemis?" he asked as he struggled to get up.

"Gone," Clancy said. He pushed him back down.

Grass tickled his neck. "What do you mean, gone!" He rose up on elbows and looked around.

Clancy had a goose egg forming on his forehead. "The Leader took her at knifepoint. The Runners are following, but they cannot overtake him for fear that he'll harm the lady."

Brian pulled off his mask with disgust. "How long have I been lying here?"

"Nearly ten minutes. I just came to myself. I beg your pardon for not keeping her safe." He hung his head.

Brian stood with a groan and nearly cast up his accounts. "The fault is mine, Clancy, not yours. I thought up this travesty of a plan." He hobbled over to his fellow highwaymen, now shackled. Grabbing one man by the shirt he demanded, "Where did he take her?"

The two men, who he did not recall ever seeing before, gawked at him.

"Don't you know anything about him?" Brian nearly screamed.

One of the men hung his head in shame. "We know no more than you. No one was ever supposed to be harmed."

Brian's anger raged hot, but he pushed the man he held away from him with contempt. He had to find her! "Someone, fetch me my horse," he barked.

"Now, just hold on," one of the Runners said. "You'll bleed to death if you don't take care of that stab wound. There are six men following them. The Leader won't get far without us knowing where."

Brian wanted to argue, but dizziness took over his anger. He needed a bandage before he could be of any help to Artemis. He glanced at the carriage door, where Clancy stuck his head out.

"You are going to have to strip down, my lord, if you plan on wearing those breeches. Perhaps you'd rather come into the carriage?" Clancy asked.

Brian made his way inside, and he sat down with a grimace. Clancy helped him with his boots and pantaloons. Brian leaned back into the corner of the carriage, the rest of him stretched out on the seat.

Clancy took a good look at the wound. "She nearly made you a gelding."

Brian winced. "No doubt. Can you bandage it fast? And someone fetch me a horse!" he yelled.

Clancy lifted one of the seats of the carriage. He pulled out a bottle of brandy along with a black bag. "I'll see what I can do." Clancy swabbed the opened cut with a cotton towel. "She missed your vein or else you'd not be talking just now." Clancy whistled as he inspected the knife wound closer. "I'll give you this much, you taught her well. This needs stitching. I think the thread will stay put as you ride, but you'll have to take care in mounting and dismounting. Just so, the cut's already started to clot. That is a good sign." He handed him the bottle. "Here, drink this, it'll steady you. You're going to need it."

Brian took a deep pull of the brandy, then clenched his teeth as Clancy poked and prodded his flesh with the needle and thread. He wondered who the devil was the Leader and why would he take Artemis when he already had the blunt!

By the time Brian mounted his horse and surveyed the immediate area, he knew he was too late. Several of the officers from Bow Street returned with dejected nods of their heads. They had lost the Leader's trail. Brian had no idea where the scoundrel might have taken Artemis, and that scared him like nothing else. How was he going to find her?

He looked up at the late afternoon sky. The sun would set in a few hours. He checked his pocket watch that hung from his waistcoat. It was half past three. He had to find Artemis by nightfall, and unfortunately, he had to inform Lord and Lady Ashbourne what had happened.

Realizing there was nothing more he could do at the moment, Brian carefully dismounted and tied his horse to the back of his carriage, then he climbed inside with Clancy, grabbed the bottle of brandy, and took a deep swig. "We have to find her," he said when he handed the bottle back.

"We will, my lord."

Brian opened the trap and gave his coachman orders to go directly to Lady Ashbourne's townhouse in Mayfair. From there he would go directly to Bow Street to review the reports with John Stafford and see if there was any clue he had missed.

He settled his head against the leather squabs and closed his eyes, throwing his arm across his face. He had set up this entire charade to avenge his brother's death and bring the highwaymen to justice. He had blundered miserably.

Although two men had been caught, the most important villain had gotten away. He had taken with him the woman Brian loved and promised to protect. He had failed her this once; he would not fail her again.

Chapter Twelve

$\mathcal{A}$rtemis struggled for a smidgen of comfort. The weight of her captor as he lay nearly on top of her made it hard to breathe. He pulled the blade against her throat even harder, causing her to cough and sputter.

"Keep quiet or I will slice you and leave you to die," he whispered into her ear.

She shivered with fear. They were in a hole beneath a huge oak tree. She lay on her belly, and the smell of dirt filled her nostrils, since her face was practically pushed into the soil. She stilled every aching muscle and calmed her uneven breathing in order not to make a sound. If her kidnapper acted on his threat, she would never be found.

"Pretty little hideout would you not say?" he continued to whisper in her ear. "I found it the day I stole your ring. It has since served me well."

She heard the rustling sounds of the Runners searching for them. She longed to cry out for help, but instead she shut her eyes tight, forcing herself to remain quiet. The villain held her more firmly as if reading her very thoughts. Cherry, she thought with utter despair. Where are you?

"Nothing here," one of the Runners said.

Artemis stifled a sob that rose in her throat when she heard the men leave. She had never felt so alone in her life. She was completely on her own.

"They'll never find my horses," he hissed. "Another ingenious stroke of luck I stumbled upon. We need wait only a few moments more until they have gone."

Artemis rested her forehead upon the ground. Did he want her to congratulate him on his criminal mind?

It seemed like hours before the Leader finally crawled out of his hole, dragging her with him. As much as she loathed the closed-in feeling of laying under a tree's roots, she did not relish going anywhere with the masked man that pushed her along, dagger still poised against her neck.

The sun had fallen low in the western sky, casting an eerie orange glow through the woods. Artemis worried about Miranda and Ashbourne. What must they be thinking? Did they have any idea what had happened to her? Had they looked for Cherry? Why did she not see him with the Runners this afternoon?

She swallowed the questions that made her sick with wondering and worry. She must think more positively. Cherry would come for her eventually, he had to. In the meantime, she needed to do whatever she could to help him find her.

As they walked through the dense forest, she racked her brain for ideas how to alert searchers of her presence. Her hands swished along the sides of her skirt, when it dawned on her. She reached into the deep pocket of her gown and found the lace mitten.

She silently dropped it upon the ground. She held her breath, hoping the Leader had not noticed. After no outburst from the man, Artemis breathed a little easier.

While they walked, Artemis contemplated how she might get away. The Highwayman could hardly keep a dagger at her throat while he mounted his horse, she thought. She needed to bide her time until the opportunity to escape presented itself. When he retrieved his horse, she must act quickly.

They came upon a clearing with a small farm nestled in the open meadow. Children played near a large mud puddle with a tiny sailboat they pushed into the brown water. Artemis' knees grew weak with relief. Surely these people would help her.

"Cor, what'ya got there, govna?" a small man with no teeth said when he walked out of the barn. Her hope shriveled and died. The farmer did not care a whit. Instead, he acted amused by her predicament.

"A souvenir from my latest holdup," the Leader said as he flipped a gold crown to the man. "And she is a feisty one at that. I might decide to make her my missus."

"I'll 'ave yer buggy brought round." The farmer winked then returned to the barn.

"You cannot do this," Artemis choked out. Her fears deepened when she saw the carriage. She would have no hope of escaping now.

"And who will stop me?"

"Lord Cherrington." She lifted her chin with scorn.

"He accompanied the Runners this afternoon. He will see to it that you are caught and punished for this."

The Leader laughed harshly. "That popinjay? I did not see him. Are you sure he was not hiding from fright? The man is a coward, just as his brother before him."

"You killed his brother," Artemis spat.

"The fool killed himself." He shoved her roughly against the carriage that stood before them.

Artemis fell to her knees, and her eyes widened. The carriage was crested, but she did not have a clue to the identity of the crest. Had she seen this very same carriage at a rout or ball? Dread ate away at her already ill stomach. She looked at the man who roughly brought her to her feet and thrust her inside. "Who are you?" she asked.

"All in good time, my dear," he drawled and sat down across from her.

Brian was shown into the drawing room by Lady Ashbourne's formidable butler, whose expression revealed extreme disapproval over Brian's appearance. He had not bothered to change, and the cloying smell of dried blood hung on him.

He did not wish to waste time, but Lord and Lady Ashbourne must be informed of the situation. Clancy had dropped him off and would return with two fresh mounts for them to renew the search.

During the half hour carriage ride back to Town, Brian ran through the events of the holdup over and over. He wondered why the Leader had demanded that Artemis hand him the pound notes. Why had he stalled? He had the funds in hand, so to speak, after Brian took the bag from the basket. Why require Artemis to hand over the blunt?

Brian had acted poorly by grabbing Artemis from behind in an attempt to throw her into the carriage. He had misjudged her speed of action in defending herself. He only wanted her safe and away from the Leader, but instead he had made a complete mull of things. He should have told her that he had been acting with the highwaymen. Had he confided in her, trusted her with the knowledge, this might not have happened.

Brian's mind raced furiously. The Leader had used Artemis as a guarantee of his escape, but he had lured her to his side well before the Runners had appeared almost as if he had expected them.

The letter!

All this time he had thought Artemis the author, when it could have been the Leader. He had to get to Bow Street!

"Lord Cherrington?" Lady Ashbourne looked confused as she stepped into the drawing room.

Her husband followed, his scowl deep. "You're looking different than usual," Ashbourne said with barely concealed disdain. "Where is Artemis? She left a note that she was with you."

"I can explain," Brian started. He ran his hand through his hair, wondering where to begin. "Artemis has been kidnapped by the Leader of the band of highwaymen who have been attacking nobles."

Lady Ashbourne gasped and collapsed onto the divan. "They have the Rothwell ring; now they have Artemis!"

Brian nodded. "Indeed."

"Someone please tell me what is going on?" It was Ashbourne's turn to look confused and also furious.

"Artemis and Beatrice were robbed by the highwaymen before the Season, and the Rothwell ring was stolen," Lady Ashbourne said quickly, unshed tears shining in her fine eyes.

"Why didn't you tell me?" Ashbourne asked.

"Because, I promised Bea. If Rothwell found out, Artemis would have been sent home immediately, her come-out canceled."

Ashbourne shook his head as if to clear it from female rationalization. "Instead he will have our heads for not protecting her." He turned to Brian. "What has this to do with you?"

"The fault is entirely mine." Brian stiffly stood. "I have been working with Bow Street in an attempt to bring these bandits to justice. I planned a trap to capture the thieves using Artemis as the bait, an exchange of pound notes for the Rothwell ring." Brian could no longer meet Ashbourne's gaze. He felt lower than dirt.

"There was an advertisement in the *Post*—" Ashbourne's eyebrow rose.

"Mine. I placed it, with Artemis' consent of course, but that is neither here nor there. Ashbourne, we waste time arguing. I am straight for Bow Street. I promise I will find her."

"Not without me, you won't," Ashbourne said. "Can you ride?" he asked when he noticed Brian's limp.

"My horse is out front."

"Very well, I will join you momentarily." Ashbourne turned to his wife.

"Meet me at Bow Street and ask for John Stafford. I will be with him." Brian started for the door. He did not wait for Ashbourne's agreement. In no time he and Clancy galloped through Mayfair toward Bow Street.

Brian entered John Stafford's office without the formality of being addressed. "Where is the letter informing you about the time and place of the North Road holdup?"

Stafford narrowed his gaze before pulling out the piece of parchment. "Lord Cherrington, you are wounded and upset. Please understand that we have every available man looking for her."

Brian ignored him and read the letter. He berated himself for assuming it was written by Artemis. "Was there no envelope? No seal?"

"Only that," Stafford said. "Delivered by a boy of the streets."

The Leader often used street urchins to deliver his messages. Brian was certain the letter had come from him. Which meant the Leader wanted his men caught and arrested.

Ashbourne entered the chief clerk's office with a nod and brief introduction to John Stafford.

Brian held out the letter for Ashbourne to view. "Do you know Artemis' handwriting? Could this be hers?"

Ashbourne shook his head. "No. Her hand is much neater and not so far slanted."

Brian gritted his teeth to keep an oath from escaping his lips. He had miscalculated on all counts. He thought himself very clever indeed to create a trap for his fellow bandits. Instead, their Leader had turned the tables and laid a snare for them all, including Artemis. He had planned to kidnap her all along, Brian would bet a monkey on it. He turned to Ashbourne. "Who might wish Artemis harm?"

Ashbourne looked shocked. "No one that I know."

Stafford rose to his feet. "Lord Cherrington, are you saying that the Leader planned this as a way to punish Miss Rothwell?"

"That and perhaps end his criminal career with no one left as witness against him. Who are the two men captured?"

"Mr. Dollins and Lord Ellington," Stafford said.

Brian was not familiar with either gentleman.

"Reprobates, the both of them." Ashbourne's lip curled with distaste. "They ran with the gaming crowd, although where I encountered them was on the field a time or two at Quorn. They follow their own rules, not caring if they destroy a farmer's hedgerow or a good hunter."

Brian paced awkwardly. The identity of the Leader was there, he could smell it, if only he could fit the pieces together. This band of gentlemen thieves had been created with a purpose other than simply stealing from the nobility, he'd swear by it. "Who might have something to gain from the ruin of these men?" Brian asked Stafford and Ashbourne.

Both looked at him in confusion.

"I cannot help but think this farce of highway robbery was nothing more than a grand scheme of revenge. And Artemis Rothwell was also made a target of our Leader's wrath. Who might have a connection to Dollins and Ellington as well as to Rothwell? Might there be a connection through foxhunting?"

Ashbourne scratched his chin. "Rothwell does not rub elbows with the likes of either men. The only enemies Artemis has according to Lady Ashbourne are the Waterton-Smythe sisters. They have tried to discredit Artemis at various functions since the Season began. These sisters attended the Rothwell house party during the Quorn, but neither of the men captured were there."

Brian nodded. Ashbourne knew little more about London society than he did. "I wonder if our Leader was a guest then?"

"We did have some trouble with Rothwell's horses falling ill. I thought it was Osbaldeston's doing, but I could never prove it. My wife had been injured in a riding accident, and I lost my appetite for seeking out the cur. But Osbaldeston, who should never have been the Master of the Quorn, in my opinion, is merely jealous of Rothwell's stock. He has not the energy for a scheme like this. He is far too lazy."

"And still in the Shires," Stafford added. "Even so, I will send a runner to his home here in Town."

Brian opened his mouth to ask more about the Rothwell hunting party when a Runner burst into Stafford's office holding out a lacey mitten.

"I say, Mr. Stafford, we found this off the North Road. There's a small farm not far from where we found the glove, but the farmer swore he had not seen a thing."

Brian grabbed the mitten and brought it to his nose. He inhaled deeply. A trace of Lily of the Valley, the scent Artemis wore, lingered. It had to be hers. He looked at the Runner. "Take me where you found this."

* * *

Artemis closed her eyes as the carriage swayed and dipped over rough back roads. "Where are you taking me?"

"A surprise," he said.

"*Why* have you taken me? You have your money, why kidnap me?" she asked. Weariness had replaced her fear. He no longer threatened her with the dagger. He did not need to. They traveled at a good pace across the countryside considering they did not use the toll roads. Besides, the carriage door had been locked from the inside, and her captor held the key. There was no way for her to escape.

"You shall see in good time, my giantess," he purred. He had not taken off his mask, and that bothered her far more than the sneering remark about her size.

He cocked his head, his brown eyes gleaming through the slits in his mask. "You are not quite as disagreeable to look upon, especially with your hair falling about your face."

Artemis seethed as he boldly gawked at her.

"Your figure is fine even if you are far too tall for my taste. I like my ladies dainty," he said with a sneer.

"And weaker, no doubt," Artemis growled. She did not like this turn of events one whit. She did not appreciate his licentious expression.

His bark of laughter filled the carriage. "I had always thought that was preferable, but perhaps I was wrong. You promise fire at least."

Artemis swallowed the panic that threatened to choke her. She could not appear weak for even a moment. She would not allow this man to rattle her so. "Tell me what happened to Lord Cherrington's brother, Charles."

The Leader was caught off guard by her question, but then a slow smile spread across his face. "I never intended for the man to be hurt, but then he was a fool who got what he deserved in the end. He was a drunken fool who pissed on himself after we stopped his carriage."

Artemis cringed. Perhaps she had not been wise in her choice of conversation. She suddenly did not want to hear the sordid tale. But she could not ignore his words.

"Once his servants had been tied and subdued, we called the infamous Lord Cherrington out of his carriage. A man who openly kept several mistresses deserved to be robbed in my opinion. Humiliated, even. How could the mighty *ton* overlook such horrendous transgressions? Why even the matchmaking mamas paraded their sweet innocents in front of that whoremonger just for a piece of his title and wealth. For shame."

Artemis felt the hairs of her neck stand on end. Dear Lord, she thought helplessly, he was mad.

"I toyed with the fool until he sobbed like a baby. He threw himself at me, begging for mercy, and my pistol went off. I never intended to kill the wretch."

Artemis felt deep sympathy for Charles. And even more sorrow for Cherry. He would indeed be upset once he knew how his brother had died. Such an account would not ease the ill feelings Cherry carried guiltily toward his brother. It could not help that Charles had not died well.

"You see my dear, there is one thing I cannot

abide." He placed his elbows upon his knees and leaned toward her. "I loathe those that flout society's conventions without suffering the consequences. A man of nobility should act with honor, and a maid should act feminine." His eyes glittered with malice, his meaning very clear. He did not approve of her athletic skill, or the *ton*'s acceptance of it.

Her breath caught in her throat, but she coughed to clear it. "You have provided a grand example of honor by stealing and kidnapping."

His eyes narrowed behind his mask. "I seek only to get even, my dear, as is my right."

"Even?" Artemis snorted the word. "For what? What have I ever done to you?"

"Come now, Miss Rothwell," he said. "You make a spectacle of yourself by beating gentlemen at much more than parlor games. You accepted then immediately jilted Lord Ashbourne for no reason and received naught a scold. If the *ton* were to know that you once rode in the Quorn dressed as a man—*tsk, tsk.*" His gaze sharpened with anger. "You have disgraced yourself time and again, yet you continue to smell like a hothouse rose among the natural blossoms of the haute monde. Tonight, I will correct that error, and save society from your odious presence."

Artemis shivered. Who was this man and how did he know that she had ridden at Quorn? "Were you a guest at Rothwell Park for the house party?" She racked her memory of the guest list for any clue to the identity of her captor.

"Never an invitation and yet I ride the Shires every year, and I have purchased a hunter or two from your father."

"I am dreadfully sorry," she started, hoping to calm the raging madness that emanated from him like strong perfume. It made her ill and desperate to be away from him. "I am certain your invitation was overlooked . . ."

"Nice try, Miss Rothwell. But you see, I am held in contempt and kept from the best houses for no other reason than the actions of my father. Unlike you, I am respectable but I unfairly bear the stain of my father's past."

Artemis was confused. What had his father done? He closed the distance between them by sitting on the bench next to her. She nearly jumped.

"Do relax, my dear. I simply must fix your hair." He brushed the fallen tendrils back and refastened them with pins already in her hair. "I have a long cloak for you to wear. We cannot arrive at the inn with you looking dirty, now can we? And do smile, Miss Rothwell, we are lovers on our way to elope."

Brian, Ashbourne, Clancy, and several Runners thundered into the clearing where a small farm had settled down quietly for the night. Brian cautiously slid from his horse. His leg and hip throbbed. Ignoring the steady pain, he limped to the farmhouse and knocked vigorously.

A small man of indeterminable age opened the door. "What yer want?"

"A man came through here with a tall young woman, did you see them?"

The man gave him a toothless grin. "Cor, I 'aven't seen a soul."

"It is imperative that you tell us, since the young lady may be in dire trouble," Brian tried to reason with the man, but to no avail. He stood by his claim that no one had passed this way.

"There's carriage tracks coming from out of the barn," a Runner shouted.

The small man looked worried. He tried to close the door, but Brian's foot and fist got in the way. Brian slammed the door back against the inside wall and stepped inside the farmer's cottage. Small children seated around a puny hearth looked up, their eyes wide.

A woman, equally tiny, gathered her raggedy dressed children into her lap. Fear shone from her round eyes. "Give 'em wot they want, Tommy," she said.

"Shut it, Meg," the farmer hissed.

Brian stepped forward, ready to do battle, but Ashbourne held him back.

"Madam," Ashbourne soothed with a wide smile. "I am certain that you and your husband meant no harm in harboring this man's carriage, but a crime has been committed and the young lady is in my charge. Her father will have my head if anything happens to her. Having children of your own, you must understand."

The woman looked sharply at her husband, who now stood uncertain, scratching his head.

Ashbourne smiled patiently, dimples creasing his face, making him look most congenial. He flipped a gold sovereign onto the poor man's table. "Please help us."

"Lud!" His wife grabbed it up quickly, her children sliding from her lap to land in heaps on the floor.

"Aye." The farmer hung his head in shame. " 'E took the lady by the North Road, said he was gonna make 'er 'is missus. That masked man better not come 'ere looking to kill me. I got a family to look after."

Ashbourne bowed politely. "Do not worry. You will be safe from the villain. I give you my word."

"Did the masked man ever give you his name?" Brian asked.

"Nah. But 'e were a lofty gent with a fancy carriage and all. Said 'e 'ad connections and that I'd be snuffed out like a candle if I ever told. Paid me well for my trouble, too."

Brian exchanged a look with Ashbourne before nodding to the farmer. Who could it be? They left the farmer's cottage and mounted their horses. "Thank you," Brian said with a tight lip as he eased into his saddle.

"I did not think you could pummel the information out of the man. Besides, I wasn't about to stand by and let his wife watch you beat her husband." Ashbourne grinned, his dimples deepening into his cheeks.

Brian grimaced as he tried to find a comfortable way to sit. His stitched skin itched and burned. "You can be rather winning when you're not scowling," he said with forced good humor.

"Just as you are rather acceptable when you're not prancing about like a popinjay," Ashbourne returned.

"The North Road," Brian said, realization dawning. "That leads to Gretna Green."

Ashbourne groaned. "Then he's got compromise on his mind."

"I'll kill him first," Brian grumbled. He turned to the other men. "We have several inns ahead of us, perhaps we should separate."

Chapter Thirteen

*H*e leaned back against the carriage seat, satisfied with the fear he read in Miss Rothwell's eyes. His plan had worked marvelously. Dollins and Ellington had been caught, their lives ruined. It was a fitting end for the men who had accused his father of cheating at cards while he had been on his Grand Tour. His father had done the honorable thing by leveling a pistol against his temple and pulling the trigger, but that action had left its mark on his son's social standing forever.

Fellows, who he cared little about, lay stabbed by Miss Rothwell. A just reward for the man who had the gall to offer the giant wench a rose. He had laughed when Miss Rothwell knocked Fellows' pallid offering of admiration aside.

He cocked his head as he looked more closely at her, much to her discomfort. Her features were too strong but it mattered not how she looked. The important element was that finally she would be punished for her transgressions against polite society.

He would thoroughly compromise her with no hope of redemption in the eyes of the *ton*.

"We have arrived," he said as the carriage pulled into the inn. "I can dispense with my disguise, as it is quite important to my plan that you are seen with me." He pulled off the black mask with grandeur.

"Lord Ranton!" Artemis gasped.

"The very same." He bowed then raked his hands through his dark brown hair before placing a tall beaver top hat upon his head. He changed into a neatly pressed coat of dark blue superfine that hung from a small peg on the carriage wall.

"What are you going to do now?" she asked. Had all his nonsense about society holding him in contempt been just that? He was accepted by the *ton*. She had seen him at several functions. He had called upon her at Miranda's townhouse! But then she remembered Harriet's words that Lord Ranton was on the fringes of decency. Mr. Clasby was there too, but that was his own doing.

"If you have finished staring, my dear, might we alight from this vehicle and procure a room?" He checked the time on his pocket watch. "Considering the hour and that we arrive completely alone without proper supervision, your reputation will be delectably ruined."

Anger roiled in her stomach until it boiled over any fear or nervousness she felt. For once in her life, she truly cared about her reputation. She took great satisfaction in knowing that she had done well this Season. She finally believed that she could act like a lady and not appear a fool. This scoundrel of a man threatened to wreak havoc on all she had accomplished with his scheme of revenge, and she was not

about to let him get away with it. Stepping out of
the carriage, she let her other lace mitten drop in the
dust and bustle of the posting house yard.

"No crested carriage with a man and a very tall
young woman stopped here?" Brian confirmed with
frustration. They had split off from the Runners to
cover more ground. It was the second posting house
they had checked after several tollgates, and still they
had come away empty-handed.

"No one like that," the proprietor said. "Try The
Crown and Thistle."

Brian pulled at his hair, groaning.

"We will find them," Ashbourne said calmly.

"But we are running out of time," he said frantically. The sun had long since set, and darkness surrounded them. He kept envisioning Artemis trying
her best to fight off the Leader's advances. The very
thought made him numb with fear.

Ashbourne remained deep in thought. "If he has
planned this out, where is the most likely inn to compromise a maid?"

Brian shook his head and rubbed his aching thigh.
"How should I know?"

"Think. You said this Leader liked to put on a
show when he robbed his betters. What is the most
crowded inn near here. They cannot go all the way
to Gretna tonight."

"Sweet Revelation! The Lion's Head."

"Then let us go there at once," Ashbourne said.

"Indeed." He turned to Clancy. "Head east and
find the Runners, then meet us there."

"Righto!" Clancy took off at a gallop.

*   *   *

Artemis stepped into the overly warm taproom filled with travelers and a haze of smoke emanating from a green log thrown carelessly into the fire. Her gaze scanned every person there. She tried desperately to alert anyone who might take notice of her dire circumstances with widened eyes. But not a soul moved to help her.

Lord Ranton held the dagger firmly against her side through the ladies' cape he had draped over her. He had tucked her arm securely in his, and he patted her hand as a reminder that should she try to escape, he would not hesitate to use the blade.

Several of the gentlemen she recognized from Town, but there were few ladies she could count as acquaintances.

"Ranton," one man well in his cups bellowed from a small table in front of the hissing fire. "What have we here?"

"This is Miss Rothwell," Lord Ranton said loudly. "We are on our way north."

"To go over the anvil?" The belligerent-looking man laughed heartily. "Well now, good luck, my boy, you look as though you will need it!"

Several other men in the taproom joined in the raucous laughter. And Artemis wanted to hang her head in shame. The men laughed and raised their glasses in a mock toast. The ladies seated in the dining area and great room either lifted their noses with condescension or grinned with an experienced smirk. Her very presence here, alone with Lord Ranton, would no doubt be spread quickly by gossips.

At the front desk, Lord Ranton arranged for a

room with a private parlor. He also took the liberty of ordering their supper. Artemis had to own, despite all that had happened to her today, she was indeed hungry and looking forward to a hot meal.

She followed Lord Ranton's instructions perfectly as they ascended the stairs, still side by side, the dagger's point pricking through the cape to scrape her dress and skin. She did not trust Lord Ranton's reaction should she try to overtake him on the stairs and escape. Neither did she trust the drunken bloods in the tap.

Seeing her run from Lord Ranton, they might believe she simply suffered from a case of brides' jitters. It would be a waste of energy should she break free only to be returned to her kidnapper. She looked back at the main entrance of the inn, wishing desperately that Cherry would come for her.

Even so, her best chance of escape was once they were alone. Now that she knew it was Lord Ranton who led the band of highwaymen, he was not nearly as frightening to her. She could not claim comfort, but at least her nerves had settled down and she was determined to break free as soon possible. She would make her move once they had eaten.

They entered a moderately well-appointed parlor with a bedchamber beyond two double doors that had been left open. Artemis scanned the room completely, looking for a possible exit.

"We are three floors up, so do not get any wild ideas of jumping out of the window." Lord Ranton pushed her farther into the room. "There is a basin of water on the table near the bed. If you need privacy, there is a screen there too."

"You know this place well," Artemis said.

"I have stayed here a time or two."

Artemis took off the cape and draped it over the back of a chair. She walked into the bedchamber and caught her reflection in a cheval mirror. Her dress was torn and stained with dirt and a smear of blood. She nervously smoothed her skirt, glad the Rothwell ring rested safely on her third finger. She had to find a way to escape.

"I do not make a habit of deflowering young maidens, I assure you," Lord Ranton called after her. "I am a gentleman, you know."

Artemis said nothing, but took her time with her toilette. She carefully inspected the bedchamber. Two windows graced the wall on either side of the large four-poster bed. Lace curtains danced and twisted in the light evening breeze that blew through the opened glass. She peeked out of one of them, only to sigh. There were no tree branches, rooftop, or any other structure that she might climb to. They were indeed high above a straight drop to the ground.

Her hands touched heavy draperies pulled back and festooned to the wall with long silken cords. She let the tasseled fringe at the end of each rope slide through her fingers, her mind racing. Were these cords strong enough to tie a man's hands? She wondered.

She returned to the parlor. Lord Ranton stood near the clean swept hearth. He had removed his coat and hat, and he leaned casually against the mantel with a cheroot smoldering in his lips.

"What exactly are your intentions, then?" Artemis asked. "This is hardly the action of a gentleman. But then neither is thieving and kidnapping." She watched his eyes widen at her sarcasm, but she was not afraid. This was the man who had tripped her at her first ball. She saw now that even then he had been out to punish her.

It was difficult for her not to loose her temper upon him. She must wait until the time was right. Whether he planned on ravishing her or simply compromising her with his presence, she did not intend to wait much longer to discover.

"You have a sharp tongue that I find I cannot abide. Perhaps I was mistaken to consider taking you to wife, as I fear you are a veritable harpy who would henpeck me the rest of my days." Ranton walked toward her until he stood directly in front of her. "I need not do a thing, my dear, but keep you here overnight in order to ruin you completely. But who knows what the night might hold for us." His leering gaze traveled the length of her.

Artemis gritted her teeth, wishing she had the dagger! She had no idea where he had placed it after they had entered the rented rooms. "I will not allow you to touch me," she said in a low voice.

"Oh? And just how do you propose to stop me?" When she remained silent, he continued, "Please do not tell me that you think Cherrington will ride in like a knight errant and rescue you. He is a coward, my dear, like his brother. Where was he today? You were in his carriage, I wonder why did he not accompany you?" He cupped her cheek with the palm of his hand, rubbing his thumb along her jaw as he looked up insolently into her eyes.

She pulled her head back, breathing hard through flaring nostrils. "He was with the Runners."

An image of Cherry flashed through her mind. He knew about her using a pistol at the first holdup, and he knew about the kiss. His skin was dark under the white powder just like the tall Highwayman. She had noticed how dark Romeo's jaw had been, but thought nothing of it at the time. They both had very bright blue eyes . . .

Blood rushed from her head making her dizzy. She found it hard to breathe as the realization that Cherry and the tall Highwayman were one and the same man. Dear Heavens, she had stabbed him!

Lord Ranton cocked his head with arrogance. "Was he? I did not see him, did you?"

She scowled at Lord Ranton, feeling extremely cross. "We both saw him. Lord Cherrington and your Romeo are the same man!"

Lord Ranton's eyebrows lifted. "Devil a bit, you jest."

"I do not. We set a trap for you, Lord Ranton. And that trap will soon close around your neck when Lord Cherrington and the Runners arrive."

"Do not hold your breath, my dear," Lord Ranton drawled. "I saw you stab my tall Highwayman. I had to wipe the blood from the dagger. You would hardly stab your partner unless—"

Artemis relived the sensation of stabbing Cherry when he grabbed her from behind. She remembered hearing her name called out in agony. "I have only just put the two together," she croaked.

Lord Ranton roared with laughter. "This is rich

indeed. Whose idea was this trap? It doesn't matter, since I effectively set one of my own. You left Cherrington in poor condition, my giant warrior. If he lives, he'll never forgive you."

She refused to believe that, but doubt and fear and worry nearly overcame her. What if she mortally wounded him? What if even now he lay near death's door? She had to get free and find out! *Please dearest God*, she prayed silently, *let him be all right*.

Lord Ranton stepped away from her just as supper arrived. The proprietor laid the spread of food upon the table. Tendrils of steam slid out from beneath the silver lids covering the dishes. The aroma of roasted beef and carrots assaulted her nose, making her stomach rumble in response, but she had lost her appetite. The fear that she had hurt Cherry was foremost in her thoughts.

"Please do not trouble yourself with any noise you might hear," Lord Ranton whispered to the man as he walked him to the door, but she could easily hear. He dropped a few gold coins into the innkeeper's opened hand. "Newlyweds, don't you know."

The two men exchanged a wink and smile before Lord Ranton closed the door and locked it. Artemis knew with a disappointing ache that no amount of screaming she made would bring her any aid. Her host had been effectively paid to stay away.

"Now then, shall we eat?" Lord Ranton bowed.

Artemis roughly took her seat, not waiting for Lord Ranton to pull out her chair. He shrugged his shoulders and sat opposite her.

She chewed the tender roast slowly, but could hardly taste it. She drank deep of the dark red wine.

She poured herself another goblet full to drown the mounting unease that gnawed inside of her.

"Go easy, my dear."

Artemis said nothing. Her expression must have been fierce when Lord Ranton chuckled softly. He was the foulest man she could ever imagine knowing, and she rather looked forward to what she had planned for him.

She ate lightly and then with a flourish of her napkin, she managed to slide the small but sharp table knife onto her lap without raising Lord Ranton's notice. She let the napkin rest over her fork, next to her plate.

"Finished? But you have not eaten dessert," Lord Ranton complained.

"I shall have more of the wine." Artemis reached for it, but he stayed her hand.

"I do not think so."

She met his gaze and held it, challenging him.

"Perhaps I too will forego dessert for now." His smile spread into a lecherous grin.

Artemis took a deep breath to steel her resolve.

She stood when he did, her supper knife cradled in her hand inside the deep pocket of her skirt. Lord Ranton's eyes took on an almost feverish glimmer that sent a tremor of revulsion down her spine. To think she had once wished for his attentions. She fingered the knife's handle. She must strike quickly just as Cherry had taught her with the dagger.

Thoughts of stabbing her beloved sliced through her with real pain, causing tears to gather in the corners of her eyes. She had to remain calm until she escaped. She could not fall apart just yet.

"Ahh, what have we here," he said when he spotted a music box on the tall dresser of drawers against the wall. He flicked open the lid, and the flinty notes of a waltz rang through the air. "Shall we dance?" Lord Ranton bowed low. "I promise not to let you fall, this time."

"You are the reason I fell," she said dully.

He shrugged his shoulders. "Indeed, but my actions gained nothing. You should have been ridiculed."

Anger surged through her, but she held back. She could not strike him just yet. She needed him closer to the bed.

She automatically stiffened when he placed his hand upon her waist. They swayed to the music, dipping and twirling until Artemis thought she might be sick.

She managed to lead him through the double doors into the bedchamber. Her stomach turned when she saw satisfaction glow in his eyes.

"Perhaps we might make a go of wedded bliss after all, eh?"

Artemis licked her dry lips. She ignored Lord Ranton's leering. The wine she had consumed made her thirsty, and her legs felt heavy as lead. It was all she could do to make herself move. Beads of perspiration formed on her forehead.

"Do not be nervous, my dear." Lord Ranton twirled her out of his arms. In one swift motion, he stripped off his coat and cravat.

Blood pumped through her veins, and her heart pounded in her ears. She would not let him touch her! She sought the knife inside her pocket, and when Ranton approached, she breathed deeply and made ready to strike.

"There now, see, this is not so very awful," he murmured as he tipped her head down and settled his lips upon hers.

She fought the feeling of nausea and jerked her mouth away from his just as she thrust her supper knife into his stomach. She let go of the blade when she heard his shrill scream. He doubled over, cursing fluently.

Quickly, she pushed him down onto the bed and pulled the drapery cord from off the wall with shaking hands. Lord Ranton struggled to get up. In a panic, she grabbed the large vase filled with spring flowers from the bedside table. She smashed it hard over his head and pushed him down again. He tried ineffectively to grab her before he fell back in a stupor. She wrapped the cord tightly around his wrists and pulled the ends together to tie him securely to one of the bed posts.

He came round and jerked furiously against the silken bonds that held him captive. He yelled for help, and Artemis smiled.

"No one will come for you, you cad," she hissed. "You paid the innkeeper well to stay away."

His eyes widened. "You will never recover from this, my giantess, never! You think you have won, but you are quite ruined."

She wiped her forehead with the back of her hand and noticed that her palm was covered with blood. She swallowed distasteful bile and ran from the room, slamming shut the double doors.

She scraped the dining chair across the floor and

jammed it underneath the doorknob. Lord Ranton no longer screamed for help, but he cursed her with words she had never before heard.

Little stars formed at the edges of her sight as she haltingly walked across the parlor floor. She heard a knock, then pounding, and a man called out her name. The parlor door burst open.

It was Ashbourne and—Cherry!

Brian took one look at Artemis' white face and feared the worse. "I'll kill him," he ground out.

"Cherry?" she whispered.

He saw the bloodstains on her dress and hand, and he wrapped his arms around her just as she dissolved into a fit of hysterical sobs.

"Shhhhh," he whispered. "I'm here now. He didn't—" his voice cracked—"hurt you?"

She shook her head and relief flooded his being. He jerked his head toward the bedchamber door for Ashbourne to check inside.

"No!" Artemis shouted through tears. "Lord Ranton is tied up, but I do not know if the cords will hold. I stabbed him with a table knife, but the wound is not mortal." She was rambling.

Ashbourne's eyes grew wide. "Egads, Artemis!" He shook his head. "I should have guessed Lord Ranton, the cur. He's been up to no good since I met him at the Shepeshead assembly rooms last October."

"Strike hard and fast," Artemis said on a hiccup, ignoring Ashbourne. "Just like you taught me."

Brian smiled and squeezed her tighter. "Yes, I've experienced just how well you do that, my love." He nearly laughed when he saw the horror on Ashbourne's face. He had quite a lot of explaining to do, but it did not matter. Artemis was safe and the Leader had been caught by his own dear love's capable hand.

Clancy arrived with the Runners. The men entered the bedchamber with guffaws and snorts of laughter when they found a snarling Lord Ranton tied to the bedpost, hurling insults at the she-devil named Artemis Rothwell. Brian remained where he was, calming his triumphant Amazon until her tears and trembles subsided.

Artemis could have remained in his embrace for hours, but something bothered her. She pulled away and searched his chest and shoulders with her hands kneading his body. "Where did I strike you? Where are *you* hurt?" She looked closely at him. He did not look like a man in pain.

He pulled away his coat to reveal his torn and stained pantaloons. His grin was wide. "Just missed me, you did," he said with a wink. "But I remain willing and able to produce heirs."

She understood his meaning completely and felt faint. The fuzzy stars swirled in on her again. "I could have killed you!" she muttered with her hands pressing against her temples.

"But you did not," he said with a chuckle and took her into his arms again.

Chapter Fourteen

Artemis paced the floor of the drawing room while Miranda and Harriet looked on, their amusement and concern showing with an occasional smile or a cluck of encouragement. Cherry was closeted with Ashbourne in his study, and the two men had been in there for over an hour.

Artemis stopped pacing in order to give words to her nagging thoughts. "He singled me out from the very beginning, Miranda. What if the only reason he had anything to do with me was in order to use me for his trap? He admitted as much to me. He was the tall Highwayman all along!"

"Artemis, you are way off, dear. It is quite plain to see that Lord Cherrington adores you. His eyes light up as soon as he sees you. That man has been surrounded by females this Season, and yet 'tis you that he chose to spend considerable time with."

"It is indeed true, Artie," Harriet said. "He truly cares for you, I know it and deep down you do to."

Artemis rolled her eyes. Neither of them understood. "But he needed me to entice the Leader for an exchange of the Rothwell ring."

"Oh, piddle," Miranda snorted. "He could not have had all that planned so far in advance."

"Could he not?" Artemis threw herself in a chair with a huff. After her harrowing adventure with Lord Ranton, she had been tucked into a carriage and practically cradled in Cherry's lap. His expression had been soft when he looked at her, but it had also been full of regret. She had been too tired to make sense of his charade and the part she had played in it. She fell into an exhausted sleep only to wake late this morning.

"I think you are making more of this than you need to, Artie," Harriet said as she sipped her tea.

Artemis sighed with resignation. "Perhaps you have the right of it. Even so, I can only wonder what the tabbies will make of this. Lord Ranton placed me in a compromising position, with several witnesses to verify that we were completely alone."

"Never mind all that," Miranda said with the wave of her hand. "It will be water under the bridge in no time."

"For another lady perhaps, but me? If Lord Ranton felt I was an abhorrent example of a well-bred miss, than how many others of the *ton* agree with him? This might serve to deepen their disgust."

She did not voice her deepest fear that Cherry might be put off by her tarnished reputation. He hated that his brother had brought shame to the Cherrington name. Would she embarrass him with this latest mishap?

"But it was not your fault," Harriet rose to her defense.

"Does it really matter?" Artemis felt weary of London and its strict rules of conduct.

"Artemis, all will work out in the end, you shall see. Lady Jersey sent a note only moments ago asking after your welfare. She genuinely cares about you as do many others," Miranda said. "The opinions of those who matter remain strong."

"My parents will soon know." Artemis hung her head. Ashbourne had sent a footman to Rothwell Park at first light. She was glad that Lord Ranton had been thrown in Newgate before her father could get a hold of him. This was just one more worry for them, one more problem with her at the center. She had wanted so badly to make them proud.

Miranda rose and patted Artemis' hand. "They will be a good source of support, and perhaps we might talk your father into attending a ball or two." She gestured to Harriet. "Come, Miss Whitlow, I believe Lord Cherrington will want a word in private with Miss Rothwell."

Artemis looked up and felt her stomach flip over. Cherry stepped aside to allow Miranda and Harriet to pass through the doorway. She stared at him, her senses reeling. Not a trace of his peacock clothes remained. Elegant subtly, she thought, described him perfectly. His face was strong with sharp angles of nose and jaw as always but without the pale powder, he looked incredibly masculine.

She was nervous as she stared at him and almost afraid. It felt as if she met him for the first time. But then she looked into his eyes. His eyes remained the same merry blue pools that belonged to her very own Cherry.

"May I come in?" he asked. His voice was deeper.

Without the high-pitched drawl he had affected all this time, Artemis found she very much liked the sound of his real voice.

"Of course." She stood, feeling awkward and shy.

"Artie," he began. "I am so sorry."

Her gaze flew to his, and her heart suffered a jolt of pain. "What exactly are you begging forgiveness for, my lord?"

He made quick work of the space between them as he limped toward her and took both her hands in his. "Please, my love, after all we've been through, do not *my lord* me."

His hands were warm and welcoming, but she could not think straight with him so near. She backed away. "Cherry," she said. "But that does not quite fit you anymore. I am afraid I do not really know who you are at all."

He did not let her go far. "Yes, you do." He stepped closer. "You know me better than anyone. Call me Brian or Cherry. I am the same man."

Hope flared in her chest. Perhaps, she was letting her sensibilities get the best of her, as Harriet had said. But even so, she needed to understand his charade as a town fribble. She looked closely at him. His skin was a good shade darker compared to many an Englishman. She marveled at how effective he had been at disguising himself. She had never once thought he and the tall Highwayman the same man until Lord Ranton had taunted her.

"Very well, Brian." His name rolled easily off her tongue. "Why did you pretend to be so different? Was our friendship merely make-believe as well so that you could use me to catch Ranton?"

"Artie, I love you. Don't be angry with me."

Her doubts dissolved in an instant, and her eyes embarrassingly clouded over. "You do, truly?"

His arms came around her, and he held her close. "Before God, I do. The first time I saw you, I was enamored with your ability to actually point a pistol at a highwayman with such unflinching courage."

"I was scared to death," she whispered.

"I know. Once I held you and felt you shaking, I knew and I admired you all the more."

She felt her cheeks heat at the memory of the tall Highwayman kissing her and how tempted she had been to return it. "Of course you knew about the pistol," she said. "No one had told you. I did not tell you. You were there to see it."

He grinned.

"But why act the fop?" she asked.

"Because I feared my fellow highwaymen might be anyone in society, and if they knew that the new Lord Cherrington was a rough and tumble fellow, they might guess that I had secretly played the Highwayman to avenge my brother's death."

Artemis nodded. "Charles' death was indeed an accident, a horrible accident caused by Lord Ranton."

"I figured as much."

She looked deeply into his eyes, gauging his mood, his desire to know what exactly happened. When he remained quiet, she decided that perhaps one day she would tell him what Ranton had told her. But not today. She would share the sorry tale only if Brian asked.

She played with the perfect fold of his cravat. "Are you quite sure that it will not bother you to be bested at archery? Or that I am not overly feminine, or that I stabbed you? Gracious, Brian, I could have killed you!" She swatted his shoulder. "You should have told me you were posing as the Highwayman!"

"Please pardon me for that. Had I explained my part, you would never have been kidnapped. For that I humbly beg your forgiveness. I should have known better." He nuzzled her neck.

"Of course I forgive you." It was difficult to remain standing upright with the sensations he roused.

"And, darling, you are indeed quite feminine." He nibbled just below her ear. "Are you quite satisfied that I am who I was only without the high shirt points and powder?"

She narrowed her gaze as she looked into his merry blue eyes. "I suppose so."

He grinned, looking devilish indeed. "Good. Now, with all that settled, will you marry me?"

Artemis deliberately played coy. "I suppose so."

"Wench!" he growled before taking her mouth in a kiss that left them both weak with need.

When he finally broke away for a gulp of air, he said, "I must speak to your father, of course. Ashbourne recommended that I ask you first and then apply for your father's approval. Do you think he will give it after all this?"

Artemis ran her fingers through Brian's hair. "You will have to learn to appreciate a good hunt, you know. But I think Father can be brought around."

"Pesky pastime," he said. "You will teach me?"

"I will teach you everything you need to know." She nodded.

He drew her near the couch, sat down, and pulled her into his lap. "I like the sound of that." He kissed the tip of her nose, and then the corner of her mouth.

"Brian, do stop. Miranda and Harriet will begin to wonder."

He breathed a deep sigh. "I suppose you are correct. Besides, we must plan our wedding. Considering the circumstances with Ranton, I think we should have the banns read."

She tipped her head, confused. "Must we wait so long?"

He nipped playfully at her thumb as he intertwined his fingers with hers. "I agree, but I will not have anyone think I married you to save your reputation. Even though I do love saving your delectable behind." He gave her a wicked wink. "We shall wait until your parents arrive in order to properly announce our engagement and then marry in June."

Artemis agreed. She too wanted the thing done properly. She got up off of Brian's lap, but never let go of his hand. "Come, let us tell the others."

"So you think your father will give his permission?" Brian asked.

"I will not allow him to refuse," Artemis said. She was immensely happy. There was nothing she and Cherry could not handle together. She knew that when her parents saw that, they would wish them well, and that knowledge made her proud. She had found her true love, and regardless of how her reputation fared, they could all take pride in that.

Epilogue

November 1819
Leicestershire

"Are you ready?" Brian called to his wife. Artemis looked smashing in the dark violet riding habit he had picked out for her. Her tiny cap of a hat sat rakishly atop the curls of her hairstyle.

"More than ready. I have wanted to do this my whole life and, well, last year, but then, oh never mind. I cannot believe I am actually here," she said.

"Neither can I," her father grumbled from atop his hunter. "But he is the master of you now, and if your husband sees no cause for alarm in riding at Quorn, then what is a father to say?"

"Admit it, Papa, you are glad I am here."

"I am that." Her father's chest swelled with pride. "I cannot say that Osbaldeston is happy to see you, since you are stealing away his attention."

"They will no doubt hear about this in London," Artemis said with a saucy slant to her lips.

"Perhaps you shall set a new rage of ladies riding

in the Shires." Brian reined in the magnificent hunter given to him as a wedding present from his father-in-law. He had named the beast Charles, since his mount was a show off at heart. He tried his best to keep the dancing monster from bolting. "You will stay near me?"

"Of course, I will, darling," Artemis said. "Do not worry, you will do fine. Just follow my lead."

"Romantic and funny—
I loved this book!"
—MARY BALOGH

SIGNET

Wedded
Bliss

BARBARA
METZGER

Signet
0-451-20859-5